Life Among
the
Dead

5 Zombie Stories

Rebecca M. Senese

Other Books by Rebecca M. Senese

The Night Killers

The Color of Blood: The Chronicles of Richard Damon

Wreck the Halls: 5 Christmas Horror Stories

Oh the Horror! 5 Horror Stories

By Howl & Claw: 5 Werewolf Stories

With a Bite: 5 Vampire Tales

Bad Ends: 5 Horror Stories

A Very Zombie Christmas

The Beginners Guide to the Recently Deceased

Daily Bread

The In-Between Series
Book 1: A Reluctance of Blood
Book 2: A Remembrance of Flesh
*Book 3: A Retribution of Soul

*Forthcoming

Life Among the
the
Dead

5 Zombie Stories

Rebecca M. Senese

RFAR PUBLISHING
TORONTO, CANADA

Published 2015 by RFAR Publishing
Toronto, Canada
http://www.RFARPublishing.com

This is a work of fiction. All characters appearing in this work are fictitious. Any resemblance to real persons, living or dear is purely coincidental.

Trade paper edition designed by Rebecca M. Senese
in InDesign CS5.5

Electronic editions designed by Rebecca M. Senese

Cover design: Rebecca M. Senese
Cover Image © nasu84 / SXC.hu
Interior Images © pashtet8286 / DepositPhotos.com
Xelissa / DepositPhotos.com

ISBN: 978-1-927603-25-3

Life Among the Dead

Dead

5 Zombie Stories

Table of Contents

INTRODUCTION

Zombies.

Shambling, decaying, mindless, relentless monsters. What's not to love?

Welcome to *Life Among the Dead*, a zombie story anthology.

Some people think zombies are boring. Others find them endlessly fascinating. For me, zombies connect to my love of post apocalyptic stories. There's always something interesting about reading stories about the end of the world, especially from the safety of my living room. And although zombies as such tend not to have a lot of character to them (after all, how much character can you have when your mind is, ahem, consumed with the drive to consume others), I am interested in the people who respond and survive in a world of zombies. Some learn to fight, some learn to adapt and some learn to thrive.

So enjoy these five tales of zombies and find out how these folks find *Life Among the Dead*!

Rebecca M. Senese
December 2013

Family Business

"Get a move on, they aren't gonna raise themselves!" Jeb pulled on his thick leather gloves. The stitching on the thumb of the right hand looked frayed. Darn that Lenvo, never did a proper repair job in his life. Jeb'd have to deal with that later.

"Come on, Ryan, let's go!"

Thudding sounded on the wooden stairs. Ryan appeared in the doorway, slouching on his canvas jacket.

"Just about ready, Pa."

"You are not wearing that," Jeb said. "Get a proper coat. That thing's too light."

"It's hot out there," Ryan said.

"I don't care how hot it is. Get a decent coat or you ain't coming with."

Ryan grumbled as he trooped back up the stairs. He returned a moment later, shrugging on his old leather winter coat.

"I'm boiling in this, Pa," he said before Jeb even opened the door.

"That's what you get for wasting all your money on the Grayson girl." Jeb held the door as Ryan slipped past him. Even in the darkness of the late night Jeb could make out the frown on his son's face. Sometimes the truth irritated like a tick bite.

"Ain't nothing wrong with her."

Jeb ignored his son's grumbling and picked up the shovel from beside the door. The boy followed him as he headed down the porch stairs. The breeze blew cool but the night still held onto the day's heat, unwilling or unable to give it up. Ryan would soon be sweating buckets in that coat but better sweat than contamination.

Jeb hoisted the shovel into the truck bed. "You fill up the pack yesterday like I tell ya?"

"Sure," Ryan said. He flapped the front of his coat as he walked around the truck to the passenger's side.

"Hmpf." Jeb unhooked the back of the truck and pulled the pack out.

"Pa!"

Jeb ignored his son's protest and opened the pack. A quick once through showed that Ryan had indeed replenished the pack yesterday. Wonders never ceased. Maybe, just maybe the boy listened on occasion.

He stowed the pack and closed the back of the truck. Returning to the driver's side, he slipped in beside Ryan, ignoring the boy's frown.

"Let's go," he said and started the truck.

It didn't matter how many times Jeb drove to the cemetery, he always crossed himself as he steered the truck through the broken gate and over the cracked asphalt. Used to be a time when the grounds here were kept well trimmed, green grass weedless and perfect as far the eye could see. Now the elements had taken over with wild abandon. Trees once grown tall and straight seemed to twist and bend across the land. Grass grew wild, more yellow and brown than green. Jeb's sniffles told him there was more pollen this year than last. As he stopped the truck at the edge of the pavement, he heard croaks and hisses over the ticking of the cooling engine. An owl hooted in the distance.

Ryan jumped out and headed for the back of the truck. With practiced ease, he unpacked the harnesses. Three in all. Going to be a busy, and profitable, night. Good thing too, Jeb thought. With this drought, his farming business wasn't what it should be.

Thank goodness for the raising.

Jeb hoisted the pack on his shoulder, grabbed the two shovels and nodded at Ryan. The boy had the harnesses draped across his back, perfect for proper weight distribution. Jeb pointed and they headed west.

The first graves showed signs of disruption. Jeb ignored them. Nothing good left there anyway.

The edges were always the first to go. Kids, family members, curiosity seekers, all tried their hand and made a general mess of things. The farther into the cemetery, the better. Less chance of spoilage.

After fifteen minutes of walking, Jeb signaled to Ryan. He heard a grunt as Ryan dropped the harnesses on the ground. In front of them, the tombstones reflected dull grey in the light of the half moon, like the lower nubs of an old man's teeth. Even without looking closer, Jeb figured these were old graves, probably seventy to a hundred years old. He brushed dirt off the closest one and felt the fine grit of the stone. Perfect age. Should be a good raising.

From the pack, Jeb pulled out the searcher stick and started walking around the graves, moving in an ever widening circle. The stick lay limp in his hand. Then on the fourth pass, he felt the tell tale quiver run up his palm and his forearm. He slowed his pace. The quiver increased until the stick jerked in his hands.

"Looks like a good one," Ryan said.

"Yeah." Jeb kicked at the ground, marking the spot. Then he returned the stick to the pack. He and Ryan picked up the shovels and moved to the spot. Jeb dug the shovel into the ground, hauling out a load of dirt. Ryan hung back.

"I'm really hot in this coat," the boy said.

"I'm not doing this all myself," Jeb said. "You want a share, you do some of the work. Now come on." He dug out another shovelful.

The boy shrugged in his coat. The leather shhhed against his skin.

"Can't I just take it off for the digging?"

"No," Jeb said. "Get moving."

Ryan shoveled out two swipes before stopping. "It's really hot."

"With your share you'll buy a new coat," Jeb said. "Remember this when you're mooning over that Grayson girl. Unless you want to forfeit your share?" He paused in his own shoveling.

The boy grumbled again and picked up his shovel.

They got down a couple of feet before Jeb called a halt. The base earth seemed loose enough. Should be easy enough for the raising. He climbed out the hole and helped his son out. The boy was wilting under the heavy coat. Sweat dripped down the sides of his face and made his hair stick to his skull. He'd sure remember this time, Jeb thought. He pulled a kerchief from his pocket and handed it to the boy.

"Wipe your face, Ryan, and get some water while you're at it."

"Thanks, Pa." The boy swiped the cloth over his forehead as he turned back to the pack. He pulled out the canteen and took a large swallow. He held it out to his father. Jeb shook his head. After another swig, Ryan returned the canteen to the pack.

Jeb set the shovels a distance from the hole. He'd learned from experience to keep them out of arm's reach. Sometimes they raised up with a bit of thinking in their heads. Best not to take chances.

Satisfied, he returned to the pack and pulled out the supplies Ryan had stowed the other day. Together they spread the crushed herbs and ground bones in a rough circle around the open hole. Jeb stuck the stubs of five white candles in the ground at the correct points of the circle. He didn't bother to measure although he made sure

Ryan did so. Even in the dark he could see the boy shake his head as he rolled up the tape. Probably thought he'd have to measure all the time himself, Jeb thought. He'd be eyeballing it before he knew it. The boy had good sense when he put his mind to it. Just needed focus was all.

Jeb lit the candles as Ryan fetched the first harness. After the near total darkness, the candles seemed to cast a lot of light. Jeb picked up the prod and nodded to Ryan. The boy nodded back. Ready.

Holding the prod in his left hand, Jeb lifted both hands to the sky.

"Come forth I call to you. In the name of the dark father, I command you. Rise up and come forth. Rise up to my bidding. Rise up!"

He paused in the silence. Any nearby animal had either fled or hunkered down, hiding. Only the wind rustled the distant trees. He felt the wind's approach as the hairs on his forearms stood on end. The whisper of the leaves grew louder. Off to his right, an owl burst from the trees and took to the air, circling once before sweeping away into the darkness. In front of him, Ryan shifted. The harness jiggled in his hands.

"Hush," Jeb said. The wind swooped forward, swiping at his hair as it passed. It flapped the front of his jacket, reminding him he should have zipped up. Around him, the grass shivered.

At his feet, the dirt in the hole moved. Small swirls started and bubbled up as if something was pushing from beneath. Jeb kept his face tilted upward but looked down his nose into the hole. The dirt was definitely moving. Pebbles shot up, never reaching the top of the hole. They hit the sides and ran down. A spray of dust flew up, then greater and greater clumps. Jeb lowered his arms, holding the prod in front of him. Across the hole, Ryan stood ready with the harness. Any time now.

A hand shot out of the dirt. It grabbed at the air as if at something solid then fell back, grasping at the earth. Soon a second hand appeared with less confidence, not bothering with the air this time but instantly grabbing at the ground. Next dirt-clotted hair appeared. It shook from side to side as the head struggled to free itself from the clutches of the earth.

Around them, the wind picked up, making the candle flames dance like crazy. The light flickered wildly, giving Jeb flashes of images from the hole as the creature inside pulled itself up. The images jerked like still photos, chronicling it crawling forward. Dirt flew up, making Jeb cough. Ryan squinted, holding the harness up in front of his face. The wind whipped at Jeb's hair and yanked at his coat. He envied Ryan's heavy winter coat now. It wasn't moving at all.

Then the candle to Jeb's right blew out. In front of him, the creature roared, a guttural wail of anger. Dammit, the circle was broken!

Jeb darted forward, jabbing with the prod. It sizzled as it hit the creature. The head came up, exposing the gaunt, withered face. Male from what Jeb could see. Fairly big one too. He leaned into the prod.

The male snarled. Its right arm swiped out but the reach was off track and it soared over Jeb's head. Jeb pulled back the prod, then jabbed again. He used multiple blows to drive the male back. It stumbled, arms waving. Groans and guttural snarls sounded from its torn mouth. Just one more step...

Ryan slapped on the harness. Too late the male surged forward, trying for escape. Jeb's sizzling prod drove it back even as the harness tightened, holding the male in place. With a practiced hand, Ryan slipped the muzzle over the top of the head and over the mouth. A few tightened buckles and the male was trussed. Ryan attached the back lead and tugged. The male struggled but crawled out of the hole. It tried to twist its body out of the harness to no avail.

Jeb used the prod to help Ryan guide the male back to the truck. They fastened it to the back, making sure to hobble the legs and secure them. Just for good measure, Jeb locked down the arms as well, leaving only the hands free to scrabble at the dirt by the male's knees. Used to be a time when hobbling the legs was good enough but after hearing of one rip off another raiser's protective clothing and infecting a scratch, Jeb wasn't taking any chances. Let someone else deal with that when they was cleaned up, disinfected and domesticated. Not that Jeb really believed they could be all that domesticated. But who was he to judge? As long as he got paid for his trouble, it wasn't for him to say.

Making one last check of the bonds, Jeb stood up, listening to his knees pop. He clapped a hand on Ryan's shoulder.

"Good job, boy," he said. "Let's get us the next one."

The second raising was even faster than the first. A female this time, she scrambled out of the dirt with a speed that surprised Jeb. Her high pitched snarl echoed in his ears, reminding him of his beloved Bessie. He almost lost his grip on the prod as the female leapt at him. At the last minute he lifted it, hitting her across the face. She shrieked, landing with her leg pinned beneath her. Still unused to her animated body, the female struggled to stand again, giving Ryan enough time to hurry up and get the harness around her. It was a bit big for her and both Jeb and Ryan had to work fast to tighten the straps and secure the buckles while she growled and snapped at them. Even the face cage was big. Jeb roped the straps around the back of her head and then over her face again before locking the buckle. That held the muzzle in place. The female whined. The tip of her tongue appeared between the muzzle slits. Jeb turned away.

They dragged her back to the truck and locked her down a short distance from the male. Jeb didn't like leaving two of different sex alone but they didn't have any choice. They had one more raising to do tonight or he wouldn't make his bonus. After all, Ryan needed that new coat.

They trudged back to collect their gear. Jeb tried the searcher stick but after five minutes he knew nothing remained at this site. They'd have to find a different spot.

"Let's head in," he said to Ryan. The boy huffed under his heavy coat but made no other comment as he picked up the final harness. Jeb gathered the pack and the shovels and they headed out again.

The knee high grass scraped against his boots. Hulking trees above blocked out the feeble moonlight, leaving them in a deeper darkness than before. Jeb slowed his pace, making sure Ryan stayed in ear shot. His left hand tightened on the shovels and his right tightened on the prod. Most knew he raised in this cemetery but there were a few unscrupulous types who didn't want to pay for it and tried their own hand. They tended to be hostile if discovered before a raising, panic stricken and desperate if found after. That was if they were still alive.

The pack swung on his shoulder, bumping against his side. Jeb shrugged, thinking it might be slipping. Through the bush in front of him he spotted a clearing. Another batch of graves. They'd probably find a good candidate for raising there. He hurried forward, the pack jiggling against him. Only after taking three steps did he realize what it meant...

The snarl seemed to explode by his ear. Something hit him on the right, knocking him off balance. The shovels clattered to the ground. Jeb landed on his side, left arm pinned beneath him. The pack pressed against him, giving him a few precious inches from the thing grabbing for him.

Teeth snapped at his face. Rotted, decaying breath filled his nostrils, making him gag. Dirt smeared hands clutched at him. He felt it grip the front of his coat and yank. He hadn't zipped up!

"Pa!" Ryan's scream caused a momentary distraction. The thing, a young male, jerked away, head turning toward the sound before it resumed trying to get at Jeb's flesh. Jeb still held the prod in his right hand. He tried to twist it beneath him, aiming the tip at the young male's thigh. If he could just get it to jump away by a foot...

Ryan darted forward. He swung the harness, catching the male at the side of the head. It howled, lurching sideways. Almost, just another few inches. The male's hand reached out, grabbing Jeb's wrist. Finally getting contact with something solid, the male lunged forward, mouth chomping. Jeb felt teeth mashing against his leather glove. He twisted his hand, struggling to yank it out of the male's mouth. The male bit down. Teeth scraped against the leather, leaving drag marks against the rough texture. At the edges of Jeb's fingers, the male bit down hard in one final attempt to bite through the fabric.

Jeb felt something wet on the tip of his thumb. He yelled, rocking his body back. His left arm came free. He grabbed the prod and jammed it against the male. The male howled, releasing Jeb. Ryan swung the harness again, hitting the male on the side of the head. Its head snapped back and in the stillness, Jeb recognized the tell tale break of its neck. The male flopped back, landing on its side, legs bent underneath it. It lay still in the thick grass.

Standing over it, Ryan held the harness, ready to swing again but it wasn't necessary. The male was gone. Must have been an imperfect raising, Jeb thought, making the male too brittle, too easily broken. Good thing they hadn't raised it. Some idiot had done it and probably got eaten for his trouble.

Jeb stood up. His shoulders ached from the fall. He rolled them forward and back, trying to loosen the knots in his back. It helped somewhat. Damn, that male had slobbered all over his glove. He felt it seeping through the stitches on his thumb. Definitely had to get that Lenvo to do a better job on his repair work. Jeb bent to retrieve the pack. Now his lower back hurt. He was getting to be almost too old for this job. Best to finish Ryan's training soon and then draft another apprentice. Getting the two of them working, Jeb could focus on expanding the business, making folks aware of how good his raisings were compared to the others. That was something he'd been wanting to do for a while. It was time to get started on it.

Inside the pack, he pulled out a thin white candle and lit it. In the meagre light, he noticed the wetness on the leather of his glove. Not saliva from the male like he'd expected. No, it was something else. And he'd known it all along, hadn't he?

Jeb turned to where Ryan was hunched over the male, inspecting him. The boy still had one hand on the harness, holding it in a defensive position, ready to slap it down if the male moved. Good to see the boy paid attention, even with that Grayson girl causing such distraction. If he let himself, Jeb admitted that he'd been the same way with Beatrice. But that was too many years ago. He'd never be distracted like that himself again.

There were a lot of things he'd never be again.

"Ryan," he said.

"Just a sec, Pa, let me finish checking this one." Ryan wagged the harness in his direction as he continued his inspection. Keeping his mind on the business at hand, Jeb thought with pride. The boy would make a fine raiser in time. Too bad there wasn't enough of it left.

"Ryan, I need to talk to you now, boy."

Ryan finished his inspection of the male. With a grunt, he stood up. Dragging the harness along the ground, he moved to his father.

"Don't be dragging that like that," Jeb said. "You need to treat your tools with respect. They'll only work as well you as treat 'em."

"Yes, pa, sorry." Ryan lifted the harness several inches off the ground.

Jeb blinked away the wetness in his eyes. Must be a symptom, he thought. That must be it.

He lifted the candle, letting the light spill over his right hand.

"Ryan, you need to look at this." Jeb turned his hand over.

"What, pa? Did he slobber on you?" Ryan peered at the glove.

Words caught in Jeb's throat. He coughed. When he finally got his voice working, the words came out soft and quiet.

"It ain't slobber, boy."

Ryan's head tilted to one side, the way it always had, even when he was a baby trying to figure something out that he couldn't quite grasp. He'd had that same look the first time he'd tried to walk and the same look the first time he'd helped at a raising.

"What is it, pa?"

Jeb took a deep breath and felt it rattle in his chest. Strange that he'd never noticed that rattle before. Of course it hadn't been there before. Just like those aches in his muscles hadn't been there before, or the dryness in his mouth. Even seeing the dampness on his own glove made him want to chomp down on it and chew it. Gosh, he thought, it sure came on fast. Faster than he ever would have imagined.

"Keep a tight hold on that harness, boy," Jeb said. "You'll be needing it soon enough."

Now alarm stretched itself over Ryan's face, changing the boyish features into something harder and flatter. He was aging right before Jeb's eyes. How often had he wanted that boy to mature faster, now he'd give anything to keep him young.

Too late. Too late for anything.

Jeb held out the prod. "Use this. You'll need it at full strength. Doing a raising by yourself is damn hard work. You want to be prepared and do it proper. This could make your reputation in this county. Everybody'll be coming to you for a raising after this."

"Pa!" The sound tore out of Ryan as if from the depths of his soul. In the flicker of the candle light, Jeb saw tears trace down the boy's cheeks. His own heart ached to see them even as he licked his parched lips.

Too fast. Too damn fast.

"Pay attention!" Jeb said. "I won't get to tell you later. Do it right and you'll be set. And you'd better do it right, boy. You hear me?"

Ryan nodded, his head bobbing fast and furious. A sob escaped his lips but he bit it back as he grabbed the prod out of Jeb's trembling hand. Jeb hadn't even realized he was shaking but he felt the tremors race through his body now. His muscles jerked and spasmed. It felt like all the moisture had been sucked out of him and he was thirsty, so damned thirsty. His stomach twisted.

He was starting to feel hungry too.

Ryan took a step back, holding the prod in one hand. The harness draped over the other. It bunched along his sleeve, pushing the leather fabric up, exposing a sliver of skin between his glove and the coat. Jeb felt his gaze drawn to the spot. Starving, he was starving. That soft mocha flesh reminded him of the most juicy steak he'd ever had.

He managed a step but the angle of his walk

overbalanced him. Jeb fell on his side. Spasms made his limbs jerk out. He opened his mouth to talk. A moan came out. He struggled, to his knees. His gaze found the bare spot on Ryan's wrist again. He lunged.

Pain flashed through his nerve endings. He screamed as his muscles flailed. He fell forward on his face, unable to catch himself. His bowels let go and he soiled himself. The hunger wailed inside. His jaw worked, chewing on the tall grass, gathering dirt into his mouth. A filmy haze covered his eyes. Shadows and shapes blurred and he was unable to distinguish what they were, was unable to even wonder about them.

All there was was the hunger.

And the need to feed.

His hands found the ground in front of him. He lifted himself up, smelling food. Something to eat. There, it was there. Food. Feed. Must eat. Must EAT!

The prod hissed and crackled in Ryan's hand as he shoved it into his father's face. It hit right in his mouth as it opened. The stench of cooked flesh almost made Ryan gag. He wanted to drop the prod. But he couldn't. He had to hang on, had to finish. Before him, the thing that had been his father flailed and reached for him. After a moment, the prod's electrical system overrode the thing's own animation and it fell back. His arms jerked as if still trying to reach for Ryan. The stun would only last so long.

Best get to work. That's what his father would say.

Ryan slapped the harness on, rolling the thing on its side so he could tighten the buckles on the back. He let it flop back as he secured the mask on its face. It was an 'it' now. Nothing intelligent looked back at him from his father's eyes. Whatever spark of human he'd had was gone now. In the mask, his jaw continuing to work, opening and closing, opening and closing, still trying to bite, trying to feed. Until he was properly domesticated, decontaminated and controlled, he still try to feed.

But that wasn't Ryan's problem. That was a distribution issue. All Ryan did was supply. After all, it was the family business.

And his father had raised him to take over some day.

Ryan picked up the leash and tugged. Time to take care of business.

The Art of Embalming

Stacy Breaken made one final check of her voice recording equipment before approaching the monolith-sized double oak doors. Dragging her briefcase up the stone steps had been quite the workout. Although shallow, the mansion's front marble stairs were deep, making it difficult for someone with short legs like her to walk up in a normal fashion. As if it wasn't intimidating enough to be interviewing Thorton Wendall Matthews III, she had to walk up the stairs one step at a time like a child.

Get over it, Stacy, she thought, he wants you intimidated, that's his style. She took a deep breath and let it out. Already she felt her heart rate slow from the hummingbird rate of a moment before. Chuck had given her enough background on Matthews to be prepared and impressed, along with the warnings about Matthews's infamous rudeness, not that Stacy needed to be reminded of it. Matthews's diatribes were famous throughout the art world. His refusal of all interview requests was legendary for the past ten years although they continued to flow in.

Correction, refusal of all requests until now. Until hers.

Stacy brushed nonexistent specks of dust from her jacket lapels and straightened her skirt one final time. She preferred pants but the skirt had been Chuck's idea and as loathe as she was to the idea, she knew she needed any advantage against Matthews. If showing off her legs would give her that, so be it.

The door knocker felt like it weighted ten pounds as she lifted it and let it fall against the door. She winced as it hit, expecting the knocker to dent the door. Instead it landed with a solid whomp that echoed through the door. She waited what felt like minutes and was just wondering if she should try the knocker again when the door swung open.

A tall, thin man wearing a spotless black suit inclined his head. "Ms Breaken?"

Stacy stepped forward. "Yes, I'm Stacy Breaken."

"Master Matthews has instructed me to take you to the library. He will join you momentarily."

As she stepped inside, the man closed the door behind her. It swung soundlessly and sealed with a gentle click. At once the noise from the street vanished and she found herself couched in a breathless quiet. The butler gestured her through the arching foyer and down a wide carpeted hallway. Her heels sunk into the cream coloured carpeting as if it was mud. She'd never felt anything so plush. Her grip tightened on her brief case as walked past piece after piece of priceless art. Several she recognized from the latest La Grande Artifique catalogue, sold recently for obscene amounts to an unnamed collector. She hadn't realized Matthews collected other works than his own.

At another carved oak door, the butler inclined his head, indicating she enter. Stacy stepped over the threshold into the library. The ceiling arched high above her head. Circular in shape, most of the walls were covered with bookcases that rose above her almost to the slope that curled into the domed ceiling. A wall of glass lay opposite the door, huge white sheer curtains billowing down but doing little to stop the flood of sunlight from filling the room with a golden glow. The air smelled of leather and paper with just a hint of mustiness.

"Would you like tea or coffee, ma'm?" the butler said.

"Coffee would be fine," Stacy said.

"Very good, ma'm. I'll let Master Matthews know you're here."

The butler closed the door, another silent whoosh with a gentle click. She almost felt like someone in an old gothic horror movie, shut into the library, waiting for ghosts, except the streaming sunlight and cheery feeling belayed any sense of foreboding. Setting her brief case down on one of the stuffed armchairs in the centre of the room, Stacy took to surveying the books along the walls. To her surprise, she couldn't figure out any rhyme or reason in their sequence. Nora Roberts sat next to a dissertation on tribal customs in Africa. An entire set of plumbing guidebooks shared the same shelf as a full collection of Isaac Asimov's robot novels. Not at all the kind of collection she expected from someone of Thorton Wendall Matthews III.

Behind her, the door swung open and she turned, expecting the butler. Instead, a shorter bespectacled man came through wearing a grey sports coat and carrying a silver tray loaded with a coffee pot, two mugs, a container of sugar and a paper carton of milk. He hurried to set the tray down on the large oak desk that sat under the window. Just as he did so, the pot jostled, spilling coffee out of the spout and onto the tray.

"Oh damn." The man pulled a white kerchief from his pants pocket and dabbed at the tray.

He must be Matthews's assistant, Stacy thought. She hurried over. "Can I help you pour?"

"Would you?" he said. "I'm a horrid klutz with such things. Bruno had to take of something and I didn't want you left waiting."

Stacy poured coffee into both cups. She added sugar and a splash of milk for herself. The man shook his head when she offered him either container.

"Mr. Matthews prefers it black?" she said.

"That's right," he said. "The stronger the better. A habit acquired in Latin America."

"I understand he studied down there," Stacy said. Maybe she could get more background from this man, something not mentioned in the brief bios she'd managed to dig up.

The man nodded. "For several years. The rituals and customs are so interesting. Is the coffee to your liking?"

Stacy swallowed the sip she'd taken. "Very good, yes. Have you worked for Mr. Matthews all this time?"

The man smiled as he lifted the other coffee mug. "I should say so. I'm Mr. Matthews."

Stacy froze with the mug almost to her lips. "Oh."

Matthews chuckled. "My reputation precedes me once again. Good to know it's still working. Please come and sit down, Ms Breaken."

He turned and carried the mug to one of the over stuffed armchairs. He gestured to the other chair, the one she'd set her brief case in. As she moved toward it, he took the brief case and set it on the floor by the chair.

Stacy found herself dumbfounded by these small gestures of kindness. This was not the reputation of Matthews she'd come to know. Where were the tantrums, the obnoxious behavior, the belligerent refusal to cooperate. She couldn't imagine any of that from the mild man with the grey, thinning hair and wire glasses sitting to her right. Perhaps it was time to test that theory.

"I hope you forgive me for saying this," she said, "but you aren't exactly living up to your reputation."

A chuckle came from Matthews. "Of course not. My reputation is the wunderkind of a clever promotions executive and my first gallery manager. No one is interested in a polite artist. Look at van Gogh. If he hadn't been cutting off ears who would have paid attention to his artwork after he died?"

"Are you saying the artist's eccentricities

are more important than his work?" Her hand fumbled in her brief case for her digital recorder.

"Not at all, I'm just stating that to draw attention to the work, sometimes the artist has to be… noticed." Matthews sipped his coffee.

Stacy pulled out the recorder but before she could switch it on, Matthews shook his head.

"I'm sorry I don't allow recordings in my house. I thought that was understood."

"It would really help me be more accurate," she said.

"I trust your memory will serve you," Matthews said. "No recordings."

With reluctance, Stacy stuffed the recorder back into her briefcase. She pulled out a notebook and pen. "May I take notes?"

"That would be fine."

She set her coffee on the small table between the armchairs. Balancing the notepad on her knee, she reviewed his history with him. Matthews corrected small details, reminiscing about his travels in Latin America and the various cultural rituals he had observed and how they inspired his work. Her coffee turned cold as she listened, scribbling notes furiously as Matthews waved his arms, embellishing his stories. Despite herself, Stacy found herself captivated by his tales of late nights in dive bars, voodoo rituals and voluptuous women posing naked on straw mats before being retrieved by irate fathers or husbands. Looking at the thinning hair and slight paunch pressing against the sports coat, Stacy found it hard to imagine the younger Matthews engaged in such escapades. Was this all part of the fabrication of the publicist and gallery owner? Did Matthews even know the real truth behind his story anymore or had he repeated it so often that the fiction took over?

"These rituals infest my work even to this day," Matthews said.

Stacy put her pen down. "I'm sorry, Mr. Matthews, I'm having a hard time with these stories."

Matthews tilted his head. "Really? Why is that?"

"You just don't seem… I mean these rituals you talked about. The animals, the blood, the raising up. It sounds like bad fifties horror movies."

He chuckled. "I know but where do you think they got the ideas from?"

"Are you saying you believe these rituals work?"

"I didn't say that." He held up a hand. "I said they affect my work even now."

"What do you mean by that?"

Behind his glasses, his eyes narrowed. For a moment, the stern expression on his face reminded her of all the escapades she'd read about before. Maybe some of that bad temper wasn't an act. From the darkening expression on his face, she imagined he could be quite the yeller when he wanted to be. But the darkness passed like a cloud across the sun. He smiled, his eyes crinkling at the corners.

"Perhaps you like to come take a look at my current series of sculptures. I think you'll find your answer."

He set his cup down and stood up. Stacy hurried to follow as he walked to the door. He opened it, ushering her through. With a gesture, he indicated she turn right, deeper into the house. As her feet tapped onto the marble hallway, Stacy found her heart racing. Matthews never revealed his work until the entire series was ready for viewing. Unlike other artists who worked on one piece at a time, Matthews worked in groups that could contain as many as twenty different pieces. Although his preferred medium was sculpture, Stacy knew of at least two series of ten paintings depicting different rituals or reflecting different aspects of the same landscape. She'd never heard of any reporter getting a sneak peek at a Matthews' series before. Her fingers tightened on her notebook. This could make her career in the art world!

At the end of the hallway, Matthews paused at a nondescript door. His hand resting on the door knob he turned back to her.

"Welcome to my studio," he said. He opened the door, waving his arm in a flourish.

Stacy stepped into a cavernous, darkened room. Heavy drapes hung against the far wall, blocking out most of the light and darkening the shadows from grey to deep black. In the centre of the room, several hunched, distorted figures crouched or stood on small pedestals. As she moved closer, a row of pinhole lights hanging from the ceiling began to brighten. She glanced behind her. Matthews stood by the wall, turning up a dimmer switch.

She turned away, stepping closer to the first figure. It looked like a woman. Stringy hair hung across a weathered face. The mouth stood open, distorted, snarling up toward the ceiling. Hands clutched the fabric of the front of the woman's dress. Her limbs looked twisted and gangly. Even the tracing of muscles along the narrow arms appeared strange and grotesque.

Such detail. Stacy shook her head at it. She couldn't imagine the painstaking work to shape the marble. She remembered reading DaVinci describing sculpture as merely removing the parts of the stone that wasn't the stature but she couldn't imagine seeing this kind of twisted, weird figure in any stone.

Yet the details drew her in. The folds of the fabric looked so real. She wondered if she blew on it if it would ripple. Even the finger nails looked chipped, one of them spit down the middle. The sight of it made her shiver. The shadows of the way the figure twisted made the stone flesh appeared mottled at times. As she walked around it, she could almost swear the figure shifted and changed the most minute bit. The head tilted just a little more to the right and up, the left elbow jutted just a shade more, the left knee scrapped that much closer to the pedestal. No, it had to be the light and the way she circled the sculpture. That was why he had the drapes drawn, she thought, to control the light and focus that much more.

The next figure was male, on his knees, hands reaching up. Again the mouth was open and distorted as if the figure was screaming to the heavens. The stone fabric appeared shredded, great rips hanging from the arms as it reached up. The abdomen was even more concaved than it should be, as if someone had scooped out the insides. Maybe that's why he's screaming, she thought.

The third figure was a child. Head bowed over its hands as it lifted something to its mouth. Perfect strands of stone hair spilled over the face and hands, obscuring the object the child was devouring. Stacy stepped closer for a better look.

"Don't get too close," Matthews said.

"It's doesn't ruin the effect," she said. "The detailing is incredible."

"Still, you shouldn't get too close." Matthews hurried over. He took her arm, guiding her away. "You just shouldn't get too close."

The tone of his voice struck her as odd. Why did it matter how near she got to the sculptures? Was he hiding something? Some method of production that he didn't want known? Maybe the figures had been cast, not sculpted. That might explain some of the detailing. By why was he so concerned?

Obviously he wanted to control the content of her article, hence the restriction on recordings. Too bad she hadn't thought to slip her recorder into her pocket before arriving and turning it on in secret. Of course, that would have raised an uproar that she didn't want to deal with. Still she wished there was a way to capture the unease on his face.

"Can I ask you about the postures?" she said. "How did you come to decide on having so many of them reaching up?"

Her questions had the desired effect. Matthews's expression relaxed.

"I had an idea of the general theme I was aiming for," he said. He launched into a lengthy description of choosing each piece of marble, setting the lighting even before he began sculpting and the sculpting itself. He worked on each piece in tandem, first partly on one before switching to another and yet to another.

As he talked, Stacy continued to wander around the remaining sculptures, all human figures with the same distorted features, a few lying on the ground hands clutching ahead of them, others grasping up to the ceiling. A few had their heads bent over their hands, like the child, appearing to devour something. Stacy swore she almost saw one head moving from side to side as if the teeth were working at something.

She counted thirty figures in all, one of the largest collections of a single theme Matthews had ever created. A thrill ran through her; she was the first to see it. Yet while the honour pleased her she found the subject matter of the collection disturbing. Who would want one of these tortured figures in their home? She understood the theme of societal disenchantment and disintegration of the individual but she didn't think she could stand facing one of those agonizing faces every day.

"Did you find it confusing moving from one piece to another every day?" she said as she paused beside the sculpture of a man lying on his stomach, hands reaching out with clawed fingers to grab. His face twisted between a howl and a snarl.

"Each piece spoke to me," Matthews said. "I was able to listen to them individually as they told me what they needed to emerge." He swept his hand across the room in a grand gesture.

She turned to survey the room, stepping closer to the sculpture to get a better view. The heavy drape beside her moved like a wave, billowing a few inches to block her before settling down. She stepped back again, wondering if Matthews might agree to her taking a photo of him standing in the middle of his collection the way he stood now.

Something sharp clawed into the back of her left thigh.

The shock of pain made her knee buckle. She

cried out as her leg collapsed beneath her. Her knee banged on the floor. Tears of pain stung her eyes. She knelt on the ground, hands out on the floor in front of her, as she tried to catch her breath.

"Ms Breaken!" Matthews hurried over. He put his arm around her shoulder and helped her to her feet. As she stood, her left leg felt numb. She must have hit a nerve in her knee or something, she thought as Matthews guided her toward a chair by the door. He grabbed the back of it and dragged it toward her. Stacy collapsed into it.

"What happened?" Matthews said.

She shook her head. "I don't know. I felt something stab my leg." Her hand reached under her thigh beneath her skirt. It came back sticky. Red coated her fingers. Was that her blood? How?

Matthews reared back, retreating several steps.

"I told you not to get too close," he said. Anger tinged his voice. "Why the hell didn't you listen to me?"

"I did not back into it," she said. "I wasn't moving. I swear."

"You idiot," he said. "You stupid idiot."

Well, here was the real Thorton Wendall Matthews III, she thought. Living up to his reputation at last. Too bad. It would have been nice for it to have been otherwise.

"Now I'm going to have to deal with you." He turned away, slipping off his sports coat. He hung it on a hook by the door, exchanging it for a dirty smock that he donned. He moved over to a workbench where he pulled a mask over his nose and mouth and added goggles over his eyes. Next came large, industrial rubber gloves. He bent down by the end of the workbench out of her sight then stood up, carting some kind of canister with a hose and spray attachment. He turned toward her.

At this point, Stacy realized something was wrong with her vision. Objects blurred as if her contact lenses were dirty. She blinked to clean them. The lighting shifted, first brightening until almost blinding whiteness then fading into darkening shadows. The bottom of her leg still felt numb but the top of it burned with prickling heat. Pain scorched her nerve ending, traveling to her spine where it branched out along her limbs. Her fingers and toes throbbed. She clenched her teeth in agony. Her head pounded, mirroring the frantic pounding of her heart.

"Wahz happnnn?" Her jaw refused to work properly. Her tongue flopped in her mouth. Her head lolled against the back of the chair. She tried to focus again on the man moving toward her.

"Wahzhapn!" She forced more air from her burning lungs out through her raw throat. The sound of her voice, more a moan than words, echoed under the high ceiling.

"I'm sorry." Matthews's voice was muffled through the mask. "I thought they were all dry. I was sure of it. Two days should have been enough. But I did tell you not to get too close. This isn't my fault."

He bent over the canister. He turned several valves and she heard some kind of suction begin. The hose quivered at his side as it filled with... something. She couldn't see well enough to know. She tried to focus but all she felt was burning, a burning that started deep inside, moving through her organs, along her limbs, out through her skin. Fear filled her until it too was burned away, leaving only starvation, an unquenched hunger.

Matthews jiggled the spray attachment. The hose stiffened as the compound filled it. Ready to fire.

The woman in the chair screeched and lunged forward. Matthews blasted the spray at her. Inches from him, the white spray hit her, hardening as soon as it touched flesh and air. The scream deteriorated into a gurgle. Still she fought against the spray, hands clawing, reaching for him. Muscles in her legs trembled trying to force her forward. Before the spray covered her eyes, he saw no trace of thought or intelligence inside, only the hunger, the need to kill.

"I'm sorry," he said. "I really wanted to give you an exclusive. It wasn't supposed to happen. But I told you not to get too close. They're still infected."

She froze centimeters from him, her nails hooked to tear flesh she would never reach. He stepped back, continuing to spray, coating her over and over with the white compound. His own special blend. A perfect camouflage and containment. No one would ever know and no one would ever be infected again.

As long as they didn't get too close.

He'd have to give it a week, maybe two, he decided. Obviously two days wasn't enough of a drying time. He'd have to remember to tell Bruno to reschedule the exhibition. Best to be more conservative.

Finishing the final coat, he walked around his new sculpture, surveying the results. Despite his regret, he had to admit it looked quite good. Quite striking. Head thrust forward, mouth snarling, hands reaching but never quite grabbing, legs bracing for a final lunge, it all looked like someone on the verge of leaping forward. A tremendous suggestion of movement and force. He smiled in admiration at his work. He had a new centre piece for his collection. He wondered if that reporter, whatever her name was, had ever imagined such a thing.

Now she had a real place in the world of art.

Food for Survival After a Disaster, With Plates

When the apocalypse came, Gladys Murphy found herself glad to be in Glenderson for the first time since her son had relegated her to the small retirement community. A two hour drive from the big city, she knew no one would bother with the place as they strove to contain the horrific virus that spread like wildfire through the main population. In the main entertainment room where all the able bodied residents hung out (despite all having television in their own apartments), Gladys watched with the others as the first reports trickled in. Even before the first one was over, she spotted Benjamin Stokes hobbling out the door. Everyone else was engrossed in the announcements.

What was he up to, she wondered. What was so important to miss the televised end? Unable to focus back on the anchor woman with the perfectly tousled hair, she drifted toward the back of the room and slipped out the door.

Bright, warm sunlight of a fresh July afternoon belayed any horrific events happening elsewhere. Shouldn't there be at least some cloud cover for the dissolution of the human race? Maybe instead the earth was celebrating. Goodness knows the planet deserved better than what people had been dishing out for decades.

She hadn't always been so bitter but she also hadn't expected her son to dump her here like a forgotten roast. She never thought she was a clingy mother and although she hadn't always got along with his social climbing wife, Gladys did try to be friendly and supportive. But after the children had outgrown the need for free babysitting, her son deemed her no longer able to live in her own house unassisted. Enter the "community" at Glenderson where Gladys could be out of sight and out of mind.

Now with disaster striking elsewhere, Glenderson would be out of mind for quite some time.

She noticed Stokes disappearing around the far corner of the community hall and set off after him. Daily walks with Beth Moscoe kept her legs working and she was able to reach the corner before Stokes vanished. She noticed him casting a look over his shoulder and shied back around the corner. For some reason he didn't seem to want to be followed. All the more reason to follow, she thought.

Past the gardening shed, she finally intercepted him as he tugged on the door to the old underground coal cellar.

"Benjamin Stokes, what are you up to?" she said in her best disapproving voice.

He jumped as if caught with his hand in a ladies' underwear drawer. The door rattled closed as he dropped the handle.

"Nothing," he said. A frown twisted his face. Only his left side moved properly since a stroke had affected him late last year. "What's it to you?"

"You seem in quite a hurry to miss the news," Gladys said. "You have a special stash of whiskey down there for the end?"

"Hmph. Why should I tell you?"

"Oh no reason. Maybe I'll just see if anyone else wants to take a look." She took a step back in the direction of the community centre.

"No, wait!" He beckoned her to stop. "There ain't enough for all."

"Isn't enough," she said and then pursed her lips. She was never able to get the English teacher out of her system. "What don't you have enough of for all?"

His frown deepened. The wrinkles on his face folded in on themselves as if his skin was concaving into his skull. Finally he nodded.

"Okay, I'll show you. Long as you keep it to yourself."

"I promise to consider it seriously," she said as she moved forward.

"No. You promise or you don't see nothing."

They glared at each other. She used her best disapproving teacher look but he seemed adamant. Besides, did it really matter now? She shrugged.

"Fine, I agree."

He yanked open the cellar door. Rusty hinges creaked in protest as the door swung up and then banged on the ground. Stokes stopped, tensed and waiting. Only bird song in the afternoon answered the banging door. No one in the community centre had heard it. As most of them were deaf, why would he expect them to, Gladys thought. But she didn't ask.

Stokes climbed down the stairs one at a time. Shadows swallowed his shifting body. Gladys took a tentative step onto the stairs. After the bright sunlight, the dimness of the cellar looked impenetrable. She didn't want to fall. Her hands groped for a railing that wasn't there. She took another step, then another before stopping.

"Benjamin, I can't see anything."

"Just a sec."

She heard shuffling below her, feet scraping on dirt, then a click. A bare light bulb hanging from the low ceiling burst on, sending pale yellow light across the room. Still only a fraction as bright as the sunlight, at least it allowed her to see her feet and her way down the stairs. With more confidence, Gladys started walking again and finally reached the cellar floor.

She surveyed the room with curiosity. She hadn't paid much attention to these doors on her daily walks, never seeing anyone near them. But somehow Stokes had managed to collect and organize shelves of supplies that stretched along the left wall to the end of the room. Along the right was long benches and tables. Open face cabinets were stocked with tools near the doorway, then kitchenware including plates and cutlery, then shifting into books. Along the back wall, she saw several cots with mattresses rolled up. Blankets and pillows piled on to the springs.

"What is all this?" she said.

"Preparations," he said. "Knew it was only a matter of time before something happened. If not the commies, then something. We've been preparing."

"Who's 'we'?"

"Gareth Mosley looked after it before me," Stokes said. "Don't know if he started it or what."

"I don't know him," Gladys said.

"You wouldn't. He died three years before you came. It's my responsibility since then."

She moved over to the shelves filled with canned goods. Everything was organized and labeled.

"Impressive," she said. "So what happens now? We've got that mess going on in the cities. We can't move everyone down here. There isn't enough room."

"No, we can't bring everyone," he said with a shake of his head. "Have to bring the best choices."

She turned away from the tomato paste and stared at him. "What do you mean the 'best choices'?"

He slid out a piece of paper from one of the open cabinets. "Have to bring along the most useful. Got a list here." He frowned. "Mosley left it. Seems a bit out of date." He trailed one gnarled finger along the paper. "He's dead, she's dead. Mmmm."

"You can't just pick and choose." Gladys felt indignation rise in her, making her heart flutter.

"As you said, we can't bring everyone. But there should be a few more." Stokes pocketed the paper and shuffled back to the stairs. He reached by the side and picked up a long stick. As he climbed, Gladys realized the stick was a shotgun.

"You stay here," he said when he reached the top of the stairs. Before she could reply, he slammed the door shut, blocking out the after-noon sun, leaving her in the twilight.

Dust puffing up from the slamming door made her sneeze. She rubbed her nose as she surveyed the rest of the room. Surely the atten-dants must know about this place. How could anyone have smuggled all of this food and equip-ment down here without their knowledge? She stopped in front of the books and reviewed the titles. Instructions on farming and sewing. Histories of agricultural practices. Equipment upkeep. Manuals on generators. Gladys bit her lip. Seeing these books brought it home to her in a way watching the manicured reporters on televi-sion didn't. The world as she knew it was ending.

The door creaking caught her attention. Footsteps sounded as hunched figures shuffled down the stairs. In the dim light, she couldn't make out faces until they reached the floor and looked up. Beatrice Mitchell, mechanic, Stuart Rawlings, farmer, Marcus Black, scientist, and Daniel Crawford, doctor, all blinked back at Gladys. The door swung shut with a bang and a metallic rattle, then Stokes came down the stairs.

"What's she doing here?" Crawford said.

"She followed me," Stokes said. "Couldn't stop her from seeing."

Black frowned at her, his gray moustache dipping down beside his mouth. "We can't let her stay."

Gladys stiffened. Of all of them, she was the youngest, second only to Beatrice. But Beatrice had suffered a hip injury earlier in the year. Gladys knew she could fend her off, but all of them?

"You send me out and I'll tell everyone," Gladys declared.

Murmurs rumbled through the group.

"Could kill her," Rawlings said.

"Don't be stupid, Stuart," Beatrice snapped. "Like that wouldn't look suspicious. So we've got one more. Big deal. We're already light three others. Having her here isn't going to tax the supplies."

More grumbling rumbled through the group before they seemed to reach a consensus to allow her to stay.

"Fine," Black said. He folded his arms across his chest. "What can she do besides teach English?"

Gladys pulled herself as erect as her back would allow. "I can cook. And I make excellent tea."

According to the group's code, they were to remain locked in the cellar for upwards of a month if not longer before determining if it was safe to emerge. By the second day and Gladys's meatloaf surprise, the group was congratulating themselves on their brilliance in allowing her to stay.

Stokes rigged up a ham radio, connected the antenna on the roof of the community centre. Every day, they huddled around it for news. Every day, the information flow slowed to a trickle as broadcaster after broadcaster fell silent. Every day the world seemed to shrink to encompass only the cellar.

Behind the shelves on the left was a second narrow room with an even shorter ceiling. Gladys was able to stand but most of the men had to crouch. The bathroom, connected to a septic system, was on the other side of the room and the chemical smell of it permeated the small room. But as it was the only other room in the cellar, demand for its use stayed high. They even had a roister set up for everyone to have the opportunity for privacy in that room.

How very practical and efficient, Gladys thought.

By the end of the second week, all transmissions stopped. For several days, Stokes continued to fiddle with the radio, testing the equipment, checking for any stations, but received nothing but static. Finally even he had to admit there was no one left talking.

"I think we should check outside," Black said and that set off debates that raged for days. Gladys stayed out of it as they argued, surprised at the vehemence. Beatrice quoted the agreement at them, how they were supposed to wait a month. By Gladys's count they wasted a week on this nonsense, so what was another week's wait? But she knew better than to comment. Tempers were already short in the cellar.

Finally an agreed upon date came. Stokes climbed the stairs, holding the shotgun at ready. Rawlings and Black brought up the rear. Both Beatrice and Crawford hung back. Gladys considered waiting with them but couldn't contain her curiosity. What was going on out there? She had to know.

As Stokes cracked the door, dull sunlight poured in, making all of them blink. When the door swung wide, Gladys saw low cloud in the sky above. As the men climbed up the stairs, she followed, eager to see the outside again.

Fresh air bombarded her nostrils. She breathed it in, filling her lungs and only then realizing how stale and smelly the cellar had become. If she never had to go back down there it would be a blessing.

The Glenderson grounds lay quiet before them. Stokes, Rawlings and Black stayed tense, moving forward in some kind of prescribed configuration.

"Oh for heavens sake," Gladys said. She stormed past them, heading for the community centre.

"Get back here!" Stokes growled the words at her but she was too far away to hear him. At sixty-seven, Gladys had had quite enough of the apocalypse, thank you very much. If it was the end, she'd rather face it straight up, wearing fresh clothes and having a nice cup of tea rather than huddling under ground.

Grabbing the front door to the community centre, she gave a good yank. The door popped open. The putrid stench knocked her back. She released the door, coughing as she backed away. She hadn't realized it would smell so bad. She had forgotten it was August.

Shuffling sounded from inside the building. As her coughing subsided, she saw figures moving behind the glass. The door shuddered, then began to open.

Beth Moscoe came out, or something that had been Beth Moscoe. Instead of her normal quaffed appearance, Beth's hair hung like a rat's nest around her gray, pallid skin. Never without lipstick, her lips now looked faded and her mouth opened to rotting, decaying teeth. She seemed only somewhat aware of Gladys. She moaned and managed a shuffling step.

So it's that kind of apocalypse, Gladys thought. Images from some black and white movie she'd seen years ago flashed in her mind. People barricaded in a house, mindless zombies attacking, eating anyone outside. So was Beth going to try to eat her?

After several shuffling steps, Beth appeared to lose interest in her. The creature veered to the right. One of her slippers got caught on the curb, halting her progress. Beth continued to try moving forward, not thinking to lift her foot.

Were all zombies that dense, Gladys wondered. She took a step forward, getting ready to help but then stopped. She didn't really want to get bitten but this was Beth, her friend, and her friend needed help.

Besides, wasn't she just a bit tired of all of this? Maybe it was best to face it square on.

Gladys took a breath, straightened her back and stepped forward again.

"Lift your foot, dear," she said as she took Beth's arm.

Beth tilted her head at Gladys, mouth opening and closing, either in imitation of Gladys's speech or a desire to bite, Gladys couldn't tell. But at least Beth wasn't lunging forward and chomping down. A small blessing.

"Lift your foot." Gladys tugged on Beth's arm.

Finally, like a dim witted child, Beth lifted her right foot and was able to shamble forward.

"Very good," Gladys said.

A semblance of a smile twisted Beth's lips. A corresponding moan issued from her lips.

By this time, Stokes, Rawlings and Black appeared at the corner. At the sight of Gladys with Beth, they jumped forward, brandishing weapons.

"Get back, Gladys, we'll take her," Black said.

"Take her where?" Gladys said.

"Look out, she'll attack." Rawlings pointed the shotgun.

"Just a minute," Gladys said. "The only ones attacking here are you. Beth can't even think to lift up her foot properly. She needs our help. I think the others do too."

"Others?" squeaked Black.

At this point, the door opened again and several more previous inhabitants spilled out. Disheveled and decayed looking, the three men and two women shambled out, at first spotting Gladys and the others, then losing interest as they wandered in different directions. Quite pitiful actually, Gladys thought. They definitely needed someone to take care of them.

"They're attacking!" Rawlings said.

"Oh shut up." Gladys patted Beth's arm. "Stay here, dear. I have to fetch the others."

Beth's head tilted the other way as if she was trying to nod.

Before the three men could protest further, Gladys stalked off after Barney Grayson. The short, previous tubby man ambled aimlessly in a circle. He looked like he'd shrunk inside his suit. Pants normally yanked halfway up his chest now hung off his hips.

"Come along, Barney," Gladys said. "Let's get you cleaned up."

He turned to her and she saw that his left eye rolled to the outside and was stuck, reminding her of Marty Feldman was the old movie Young Frankenstein. At least Barney didn't have a hump.

At the sight of her, his mouth moved like Beth's had, in the same open and closed manner. But he didn't lunge either. Maybe it didn't actually mean he wanted to bite her, or if he did, he and Beth were some of the laziest zombies she'd ever heard of.

She beckoned to him. "What do you say, Barney, will you come along?"

He took a shambling step forward and then another. Soon he was following her back to stand by Beth.

"Keep an eye on them," Gladys said to Stokes. "Don't let them wander off."

It took her another twenty minutes to gather the remaining wanderers. She didn't know quite what to call them. They didn't seem exactly like zombies but they certainly weren't normal. Residents, she thought. At least that was polite.

"We're not taking them down to the cellar," Black said.

"Of course not," she said. "We'll take them over to the old rec centre."

The men grumbled but as none of the residents had attacked, they couldn't very well shoot them. Not without incurring Gladys's wrath.

After much coaxing, they made their way to the rec centre. Shut down earlier that year for remodeling that never happened, the rec centre smelled stale and dusty but at least it was better than the community centre. Gladys ushered the former residents inside, coaxing them to one of the meeting rooms where they ambled in random circles. She closed the door with a gentle click. None of the residents looked up.

"Good job," Rawlings said, "getting them locked away."

Gladys looked at him like he was crazy. "I'm not locking them away. I just want them to stay in one spot while I get some fresh clothes and such."

Stokes took her arm, steering her toward the front door of the rec centre. "Gladys, you realize those people aren't people any more?"

"What are they?" she said. "Do you know? Marcus, can you tell me what they are?"

Black frowned his discomfort. "Well, they are infected, Gladys. You can see it just looking at them."

"So they're sick," she said. "Shouldn't we be taking care of them?"

"They're dangerous," Black said.

She folded her arms across her chest. "They don't seem all that dangerous to me. You're the ones with the guns and weapons."

The men looked at each other. Rawlings shook his head.

"We can't condone this," he said.

"Fine. Don't. Go back to your cellar," she said. "I'm staying here."

She turned and stalked away from them, heading for the main apartment complex. With every step, she wondered what she was doing. Certainly the residents were more than just sick. The pallid flesh, the disjointed mannerisms, all of it pointed to them being zombies. But she kept coming back to the fact that they hadn't tried to attack her, hadn't even tried to bite her. Maybe there was a semblance of humanity still inside them, a part that could be nurtured and developed further. They seemed to pathetic and incapable of looking after themselves. It tugged at Gladys.

After all that time down in the cellar, after all this time at the retirement home itself, now she had a chance to do something, to help someone.

To teach again.

It took her almost an hour to find enough clothing for all of the remaining residents. She bungled them in a cart she found in Wilma Rodricks's room. The old woman would never miss it, Gladys thought.

Along with clothes, she gathered toiletries and some other household items. Finally she headed back to the rec centre, pushing the cart in front of her.

The men were gone, returned to cellar, she imagined. As she reached the door and tugged it open, a moment of fear chilled her. Would they have killed the residents after she left? She hesitated in the doorway. She didn't want to see the bodies. But waiting here isn't going to make it unhappen, she thought.

Her footsteps echoed down the hall. The cart squeaked ahead of her. At the door, she took a deep breath and with the dust, sneezed. That wasn't a good idea. Rubbing her nose, she pulled the door open.

Most of the residents still wandered in random circles. A few stood still, staring into nothingness, or at a wall. Beth stood in front of an old movie bulletin, her head cocked as if she was reading it.

Gladys pushed the cart into the middle of the group. Barney appeared to notice her as he turned toward her. Slowly the others noticed and shifted in her direction.

"I've brought you some clothes and things to clean up with," she said. "Let's get started, shall we?"

As she knew Beth the best Gladys decided to start with her. Facials wipes removed layers of grime from her face. Her skin still had the mottled gray look but at least it was clean now, Gladys thought. As she finished, she put one of the cloths in Beth's hand.

"You wipe your neck now, dear."

She demonstrated on herself. Beth's head tilted, bloodshot eyes studying her actions. Finally Beth's hand started moving, at first near her neck, then after a moment actually making contact with her skin.

"Very good," Gladys said. She started handing out the wipes to the others.

"See what Beth is doing? Copy her."

One by one, the residents slowly lifted their cloths to their neck. Barney even wiped at his face. Gladys applauded and encouraged him. His lips twisted as if trying to smile. Beside him, one of the other men started swiping at his own face.

It took a while to instruct them on removing their clothing and wiping themselves down. Gladys winced at the sight of the wrinkled, gray, mottled bodies but they were learning to clean themselves, following directions. Dressing them took a little longer. Yet once the pants were on, the shirts were buttoned, the dresses smoothed down, every one of them looked almost human again.

Almost but not quite.

"Let's look after that hair," Gladys said.

At this, Beth appeared to perk up. She shambled forward, pushing past one of the other women to get to Gladys.

"I'm not surprised you're first in line," Gladys said. "Let's see if we can tame that rat's nest."

She helped curled Beth's fingers around a brush and held one in her own hand.

"Now follow me," she said.

She demonstrated brushing her hair. Around her, all the residents brought their hand up to their head, and began a similar brushing motion with varying degrees of success. Not bad for a first effort, Gladys thought.

With all the tangles, Beth had a difficult time with the brush. The simple delight faded from her face. She began moaning as she tugged at the brush that stuck in her hair.

"Don't tug so hard," Gladys said. "Short little strokes. You've got a lot of tangles to work through."

By the end, she helped Beth detangle her hair and then pinned it up. She handed the two brushes to the others. The men had an easier time with their thinning, short hair. The other two woman, Patty Welfrom and another woman Gladys didn't recognize had more trouble but finally managed. By the end, they all looked pleased with themselves. Odd to see the satisfied looks on their gray, sagging faces.

"Very good," she said. "Let's get rid of these old clothes."

At her direction, the residents picked up the remains of their clothing. Gladys led them around back to the garbage cans to toss them away.

What next, she wondered as she led them back inside the rec centre. She spotted the dishes she'd brought along. Of course, late afternoon. Tea time!

"Let's take these into the cafeteria," she said.

She handed a small bit to each one, stressing they were to keep a tight grip. Beth clutched hers to her chest. Barney held his against his leg. With shambling steps, she led them back to the cafeteria.

Tables and chairs still filled the room although both had been pushed against the inner wall. With coaxing, Gladys was able to get the residents to pull the tables and chairs out, setting up three of them close to the windows to take advantage of the afternoon light. Making sure they were all settled in their chairs, Gladys headed to the kitchen.

An old kettle still sat on the counter along with scraps of napkins but the rest of the cupboards were bare. She was going to have to make another run to the apartment complex. Before she left the kitchen, she flicked the light switch. Dead. She couldn't very well make tea without electricity.

She stood in the doorway, looking out at the residents. They sat in the chairs, most of them straight. Patty listed to one side and Barney was sitting with his left side against the back of the chair. For zombies, she supposed they were doing quite well. Unexpected tears welled in her eyes. She blinked them away. She could help them, teach them how to be human again. Already they looked more human than before.

But she definitely had to get power.

She hurried out of the kitchen and across the cafeteria before they could rise to follow her.

"Stay here," she called, "I'll be right back."

She had a vague idea of trying to find a generator but wasn't sure she'd know what she was looking for. Well, she had said she wasn't bringing them back to the cellar but she hadn't said she wouldn't contact the cellar folks again.

At the cellar door, Gladys knocked as loud as she could. She thought she heard shuffling on the stairs below. A muffled voice sounded after a moment.

"Who is it?"

"Who else would it be?" she said. "It's Gladys. Open the door, for heaven's sake."

The door pushed upward. She back away as it swung wide. Stokes poked his head out.

"What do you want?"

"I need to find a generator for some power. I thought you could help me."

He frowned. "Wadya want a generator for?"

"I need to make tea."

"Tea? You're making tea for them?"

"Why not?" she said. "They need to learn to do it again. Just like they needed to learn to dress themselves again."

Stokes shook his head. "Dress themselves?"

"Are you going to repeat everything I say, Benjamin Stokes, or are you going to help me?" She planted her hands on her hips.

His lips pursed as if he was trying to suppress a grin. "I reckon I'd better help you for their tea," he said.

He climbed the rest of the way out and closed the door behind him although Gladys thought she heard someone else's voice from inside. She took his arm before he could change his mind and steered him away from the cellar door.

"You can find a generator?" she said.

"Don't need to," he said. "The main one's in the garage." He pointed to the building just past the first apartment, on the other side of the old rec centre.

"Will it be connected to the rec centre?"

"Why?"

"That's where I'm keeping the residents," she said. "It's the one building I could be sure was... empty."

That phrase brought his shoulders down and reminded both of them this was not a pleasant summer stroll.

"Right," Stokes said and fell silent.

Sure enough, the generator in the garage was already hooked up to all of the buildings, even to the rec centre. They had never gotten around to disconnecting it. It took Stokes almost twenty minutes of tinkering to get the generator running. Finally it coughed and started up.

"Thank you, Benjamin," Gladys said.

The man looked awkward with her gratitude. "You're welcome."

He held for the door for her as they left the garage.

"Gladys, why are you helping them? They're already dead. It's only a matter of time."

Even though he spoke softly his voice carried in the late afternoon.

"They're still my friends," she said. "They need my help."

They walked in silence a ways.

"We need your help too," Stokes said.

A faint smile shadowed her face. "No, you don't, Benjamin. I was a stowaway, remember? You had your plans laid out before."

"Does that mean you won't be coming back down?"

Gladys looked across the grounds of the Glenderson retirement community. In the late afternoon, it all looked so normal. Certainly the grass was a little longer than it should be. No residents wander among the garden paths. Weeds sprouted where they hadn't been before but for the most part it still looked the same.

"I'm sorry, Benjamin, I won't be coming back to the cellar."

At that, she turned away from him and headed back for the old rec centre. She had tea to make.

Another month passed before Stokes cracked the door of the cellar to again check on the world outside. The mid September morning held the first hint of the winter to come. Stokes's joints ached as he climbed the cellar stairs and stepped onto the grass. None of the others followed him this time. They were used to the closed in space. All of them, including Rawlings, a farmer in his previous life, expressed misgivings about being out under the naked sky. Stokes understood the reluctance but had to come out, had to know.

He had to check on Gladys.

The Glenderson residences were starting to show the lack of upkeep. One of the distant buildings had crumbled, from what Stokes couldn't tell. As he got closer, charred wood beams hinted at a fire that had probably caused the building to collapse. The beautiful, precise, landscaped gardens were now completely overgrown. Weeds choked out any flowers, blurring the edges of the squares and rectangles into an overflowing mess. Grass waved in the breeze, brushing near the tops of his knees as he hobbled along. He couldn't even be sure he was on the stone path.

Using the shotgun in his hand like a walking stick, Stokes made his way toward the old rec centre. The door stood propped open. He caught the faint whiff of gasoline and the distant hum of the generator in the garage. His old heart quickened. Maybe Gladys was okay. Maybe she'd managed to retrain the zombies into humans.

His vision blurred as he entered the rec centre. He blinked rapidly. He was not crying.

As he moved farther into the building, the scent of gasoline faded, replaced with the stench of decay and rot. His eager steps slowed. His shoulders sagged as he tightened his grip on his shotgun. He used the butt to push open the door to the cafeteria.

The smell billowed out, choking him. Coughing, Stokes pulled the collar of his shirt up over his nose. The chairs were tucked in at all the tables except for several along the window. Clothes were piled in those chairs, but as he moved closer, he noticed bodies in those clothes. Bodies slouched against the tables. He thought he recognized Beth Moscoe's bouffant hairstyle or Barney Grayson's jacket on a corpse lying with its face in a tea cup.

Stokes held his nose through his shirt.

"Gladys?"

Something shuffled in the kitchen off the cafeteria. Stokes spun, aiming the shotgun as the door creaked open. A familiar figure emerged, carrying a tray with a teapot and tea cup and saucer.

"Gladys!"

The gray face stared at him. Her jaw hung open, head tilted to one side. She shambled forward, carrying the tray. A moan escaped from her lips.

Her foot caught on a chair. The tray jiggled in her hands. The cup and saucer slid close to the end.

"Watch out!" Stokes hurried forward, catching the side of the tray before it fell. Gladys moaned. He helped her set it down at an empty table.

"I'm so sorry, Gladys," he said.

She turned away from him and shambled back to the kitchen. A few moments later, she returned, carrying a tea cup in one hand and a saucer in the other. She set them down on the table in front of him. Her hands pawed at the chairs but seemed unable to have the strength to move them. Stokes pulled out two chairs and helped Gladys sit in one of them.

She pushed the second tea cup in front of the empty chair.

"Ahhhh," she said.

Stokes took a final look around the room. Everyone sat at the chairs, dishes in front of them. Civilized, decent. Who said you had to meet the apocalypse acting like a maniac?

He set the shotgun down by the table leg and sat down in the chair. Gladys reached for the tea pot but seemed unable to lift it. Stokes moved her hand away.

"Please," he said. "This time, allow me to pour."

He lifted the tea pot and poured them both a last cup of tea.

My Girlfriend, the Zombie

Sharon was the most beautiful girl Mitch had ever seen: long raven-dark hair that flowed halfway down her back, pale skin so smooth and silky he could barely stop running his fingers up her forearm. That always made her laugh, a joyful, light sound that lingered in his ears long after she'd left. How had she ever ended up on a dating site? Men should have been beating down her door.

"I don't have time for bars and nonsense," she said at their first meeting in his favourite coffee shop on Euclid. It was one of the few independent places where you could still find a cup of regular Joe for under a buck. Of course, they were also happy to sell you the fancy lattes and herbal teas but at times Mitch appreciated simplicity. He also liked gauging women's reactions to the Spartan, ordinary surroundings.

Sharon had arrived on time and with a nod, sat down in the plain chair across from him.

"Nice place," she said. "The coffee smells great."

"It can be strong," he said.

"Good." Her eyes sparkled at him. "I like it strong."

And he was smitten.

"How did you end up on New Date, New Life?" he said.

She dumped sugar and a dollop of milk into her coffee. "I don't have time for bars and nonsense. How about you?"

"My friend Brian swore by it." Mitch shrugged. "I never thought I'd try something like that."

"I know. I was a little leery at first, you always hear about the weirdos. But I thought I would give it a try." She smiled at him.

"How's it working out for you?" he said.

She took a sip of her coffee. Her red lipstick left a perfect imprint on the edge of the mug. "So far so good."

Then she laughed for the first time, that joyful trill that lingered in his memory all through the next day at work.

But that evening the half hour coffee date lasted three hours. Mitch learned she was a real estate agent, specializing in condos in the north end of the city. She lived three blocks from where she grew up and loved skiing in the winter.

His tale about growing up on a small farm and moving to the city for computer science at university seemed to fascinate her. She asked dozens of questions about his life and hung on every word. Even drinking decaf, Mitch found himself buzzing at the end of the night, surprised when the waitress came to their table to tell them the shop was closing.

"What? Is it already eleven?" He pulled out his cell phone. Sure enough, ten fifty-seven shone out at him. They'd been here since eight.

"Oh my, I didn't realize it was so late." Sharon scooped up her purse but Mitch shook his head.

"It's on me." He headed for the cashier and settled their bill. She waited by the door. As he followed her out, the waitress caught his attention. She nodded and gave him an approving wink.

"Let me walk you to your car," he said. Feeling a little foolish, he held out his arm.

"Thank you, kind sir." She slipped her hand around his arm, tucking into his elbow. Although her flesh was cool, he felt a warmth spread through him. Even her slightly earthy scent appealed to him.

"I can't imagine where the time went," he said. Their footsteps echoed down the sidewalk. She pointed toward the white parking sign down the block.

"I know," she said. "It feels like it was only half an hour like we planned. Maybe it was some kind of time distortion."

His heart thudded. Could a woman who looked like this actually read science fiction?

"Do you like SF?" he said.

"I love Sturgeon," she said. "Clarke, all the older ones. But I love horror even more. Frankenstein's my favourite and Poe."

They launched into a discussion of books and genres that slowed their pace until it took them almost twenty minutes to reach the parking lot. Finally at the entrance, when they'd stood for five minutes discussing views on Dhalgren, Sharon shook her head and laughed.

"I can't believe it. You got me started all over again when I really need to get home."

"Sorry," he said, not feeling the least bit sorry. He couldn't remember the last time he talked to a woman who loved to read.

"Have you read…" he started.

"Stop!" Her cool fingers pressed against his parted lips. The earthy scent floated up to his nostrils as he inhaled deeply. He could almost taste her skin.

"I really need to get home." Her voice whispered. The pupils of her eyes darkened, making her pale face even paler. Her dark hair was a shadow. His hand touched her waist. She moved forward and his hand slid around to her back.

Her lips replaced her fingers on his lips.

He didn't notice the overall coldness of her

flesh at that time. He had other things on his mind.

Ushering her to her car, he extracted a promise of dinner on Friday in two days. Her hand squeezed his after he closed the door for her. He waved as she drove off, watching spellbound as the red of her taillights vanished around the corner. He stood in a daze for a few minutes before he shook himself out of it and headed home.

At work the next day Brian cornered him by the coffee machine.

"So? How did it go?" Brian grabbed two sugar packets and shook them back and forth, to get the sugar to settle at the bottom.

"It was fine," Mitch said.

"Just fine? That's it?" Brian frowned. "Did she get an emergency phone call or something? They arrange those things in advance, you know."

"No emergency call," Mitch said. "The coffee date was fine. All three hours of it."

He turned away with a smile.

"Three hours?" Brian hurried after him. "Weren't you supposed to meet for half an hour?"

"It went a little longer."

Brian slapped a hand on Mitch's shoulder, almost spilling Mitch's coffee.

"What did I tell you? That New Date, New Life site is great! Melissa's a dream. You don't hit a home run right out of the gate like that too often."

"Gee Brian, I didn't know baseball had gates."

"You know what I mean. Are you seeing Sharon again?" Brian's eyebrows lifted high on his forehead.

"Friday," Mitch said. "We're having dinner on Friday."

"And breakfast on Saturday." Brian grinned.

Mitch felt a flush warm his cheeks. He didn't want to admit how appealing that was. "I don't know. I'll see how it goes."

Brian laughed.

As Friday counted down, Mitch felt himself get more and more nervous. What if Sharon wasn't as great as he'd imagined? What if she turned out to be some kind of harpy or tried to cling to him like his ex had? By Friday afternoon, he was almost a nervous wreck, imagining all sorts of horrifying events. He took a late lunch and power walked around the block several times, trying to clear his head.

What the hell was the matter with him? Why was he getting himself into such knots over a girl he'd met once?

Because she wasn't just a girl, he finally had to admit to himself as he passed the bank on the corner for the third time, brushing past the fake palm fronds that sat out front. She might just be The One.

Settle down, he thought. It's only dinner.

He repeated that for the rest of the afternoon and even all the way to the restaurant. His hands still felt clammy as he sat in the side booth and ordered a beer. The temptation to gulp the entire bottle was strong but he managed to settle for just a sip, setting the bottle back onto the cardboard coaster. The sip helped, as did sitting at his favourite booth in his favourite Italian restaurant. If for some reason the date turned out to be disastrous, he knew he'd at least have decent linguini.

All doubts vanished when Sen Sharon appeared in the doorway of the restaurant. A pale blue dress hugged her curves. The neckline sloped down, teasing but not revealing too much. Her dark hair was clipped at the sides of her head and trailed down over her shoulders. She scanned the restaurant, expression uncertain then a smile lit up her face when she spotted him. He gave her a little wave as she headed over.

No way could a woman like that ever be a harpy or clingy, how could he have even thought that?

He stood as she approached the booth. She stepped up to him and brushed her lips against his cheek. Her earthy scent filled his nostrils. He breathed in deep and felt his entire body relax, except for one tell tale part of him. He hastily sat down so she wouldn't notice.

She sat across from him, setting her purse on the table near the wall. "Good evening, Mitch." Her voice purred and her smile lit up the room.

He didn't even taste the linguini and didn't notice how she barely touched hers.

Again the hours sped by and they closed the restaurant. She linked her arm through his and pressed herself against him, her thigh brushing his leg. He almost stumbled, finding it suddenly uncomfortable to walk.

"Would you like a night cap?" he said. His pounding heart thudded in every part of his body.

She leaned against his arm and he felt the coolness of her skin through his short sleeves. "I'd love one."

She ended up staying for breakfast after all. Although she only drank coffee.

Weeks flew by. Sharon started spending weekends at his place, bringing over a small overnight bag on Fridays and leaving late Sunday afternoon. They also met a couple of times a week for dinner at his favourite Italian place or at her favourite Sushi place. As they settled into a routine, Mitch began to notice that she didn't eat much at the Italian place. Her fork moved the spaghetti from one side of the plate to the other as she talked and she barely ever took a bite. Concerned, he began to pay closer attention on the weekends and realized she never ate breakfast, only drank from the thermos she brought over. At other meals, she picked at the food or they were so busy, they forgot to eat. He'd find himself starving in the middle of the night and sneak out to raid the fridge while she slept curled on the bed.

She didn't seem overly concerned with her weight so he didn't think she had an eating disorder. It just seemed... odd.

He also noticed that no matter what the temperature, her skin stayed cool. Even in the heat of passion she felt cold to the touch and her flesh exuded an earthy smell. One Saturday evening, as he lay catching his breath, she cuddled against him, her cheek cold pressed against his chest. His fingers traced along her shoulder and down her arm, her skin cool to his touch.

"Are you chilly?" he said. "I can pull up the blanket."

"Hmmm," she purred and cuddled closer to him. "I feel all warm and glowing."

"Really?" he said. "You sure you aren't cold?"

She lifted her head. "Why do you ask?"

"Your skin is, I don't know, a little chilly. I just don't want you to be cold."

She rested her head on the pillow beside him. "I'm fine. I'm not cold."

He noticed the tightness in her voice and she hadn't returned her head to her normal resting place on his chest. "That's good. I'd hate to think you might be a vampire."

He held his breath a moment. Then she laughed, her usual trilling laugh and he was able to breathe normally.

"You're funny, Mitch," she said. "If I was a vampire, could you resist me?"

He turned his head, presenting his neck to her. "Bite away, dear lady!"

She laughed again and nibbled on the side of his neck. The nibbles turned to kisses and soon he forgot exactly how cold her skin was in the fire she stirred inside him.

The next morning she had to head home early. A planned open house needed her attention.

"You're only allowed to leave if I can see you later tonight," he said, his arm fixed around her waist. She laughed and squirmed against him.

"Okay, okay," she said. "Come by after eight.

I'll have something special for you." Her lingering kiss left him breathless.

The afternoon dragged on until almost seven. He headed over and with light traffic arrived at seven thirty. She wouldn't mind, he thought as he rang the doorbell to her townhouse. It echoed back, muffled by the door. After a moment, he heard something shuffling.

"Who's there?" a voice called.

"It's Mitch," he said. "Sharon, is that you?"

"Mitch, you're early!"

"Yeah, traffic was fast. You don't mind, do you?"

"I was just eating. Wait a minute."

"Sharon..."

The shuffling moved away from the door. He grabbed the brass door knob and twisted. It didn't move. She hadn't unlocked the door for him. Did she have some kind of eating disorder, he wondered. Had he turned a blind eye to it? He wouldn't do so again. She needed his help and he'd do all he could to support her.

The door opened and she stood smiling at him. "I expected you at eight. Come in!"

He slipped inside and she led him into the living room. "Would you like a beer or coffee?" she said.

He caught her hand and tugged her closer to him. His fingers traced up the coolness of her forearm.

"Sharon, I have to ask you something," he said. "Do you have a problem with food?"

Her brows drew together. "What?"

"You hardly ever eat anything when we're together, you just push the food around on your plate. You don't want to let me in when you're eating. If there's a problem I want to help."

She shook her head. "There's no problem, Mitch. I just have... different dietary requirements. It's no big deal." She shrugged.

"What is it? Are you vegetarian or vegan? I can accommodate that."

She looked away. "It's not as simple as that."

"Is it like kosher or halal?"

"No, no, nothing like that. Really it's nothing."

"Sharon, tell me. You can tell me anything."

She looked up at him and he could see the pleading in her gaze. "Mitch, it really isn't anything."

"Then if it isn't anything, why can't you tell me?"

"Stop it, Mitch, just stop it!" She yanked her arm out of his hand and turned away. She stormed out of the living room. He started to follow then changed his mind. If she wouldn't tell him outright, he'd have to find out for himself. Something felt very wrong and he wasn't going to let her hide it from him. He'd walked around blindly in too many relationships. Not this time.

He charged into the kitchen and pulled open the cupboards. A set of dishes and glasses occupied the first two cupboards but where canned goods and other foodstuffs should be it was empty. Strange. He turned toward the fridge.

Sharon hurried in and grabbed his arm.

"Mitch, don't!"

Her strength surprised him. She almost succeeded in pushing him away but he backed off suddenly, causing her to stumble forward. He slipped past her and yanked open the fridge door.

Bottles of beer and a pitcher of water sat on the top shelf. The other shelves held wrapped paper packages. He grabbed open and tore off the wrapping.

At first he thought it was ground beef but the texture looked wrong. The colouring was greyer. It looked like...

"Oh Mitch..." Sharon said. Tears leaked out of her eyes and flowed down her pale cheeks.

"What is this?" he said. "Is this brains?"

She snatched the package from him and stuffed it back in the fridge, slamming the door shut.

"Sharon, was that brains?"

"Just calves' brains," she said, sounding defensive.

"Are all of those packages brains?"

She stood in front of the closed door, blocking it. "Maybe."

"That's your different dietary requirements? You eat brains?"

"It's a delicacy," she said. "The amount of protein..." She stopped. Her shoulders slumped. "I knew you wouldn't understand."

He took her hand. Her pale fingers lay limp in his palm.

"I want to understand," he said. "Please, trust me, Sharon. Whatever it is we can deal with it together?"

Her tear-streaked face lifted to his. She blinked and bit her lower lip. A shuddering breath shook her shoulders and jiggled her perfect breasts under her silk pink shirt.

"I'm a... a zombie," she said.

He cocked his head. "What?"

She took another breath and pushed it out. "I'm a zombie."

He knew she was talking, he heard the words coming out of her mouth and even knew what they were but it didn't make sense. A zombie?

"How can you be a zombie?" he said.

She pulled her hand away and sagged against the fridge. "I got infected seven years ago. None of the doctors knew what was wrong. I tried everything but I kept getting sicker. I couldn't eat any food. My skin got so loose I thought it was going to fall off. I finally found an old witch doctor who told me what had happened. He gave me a charm to stay off the worst symptoms but I need to eat brains to survive."

"Um," Mitch said. "Do you mind if I sit down?"

She nodded and gestured at the old style '50s kitchen table. He moved to one of the vinyl chairs and sat down. The padded cushion compressed under him. Sharon pulled two bottles of beer from the fridge and set them on the green table top before sitting herself. She opened both bottles and pushed one in front of him. Mitch stared at it. It had been sitting in the same fridge as shelves of calf brains. He couldn't touch it.

Sharon fiddled with her bottle but didn't lift it to drink. "You're upset."

"I... I don't know what I am," he said. "I've never heard such a thing before." He finally looked over at her pale face. "How can you be sure you're a zombie?"

"I've had... tests," she said. "They confirm what I'm saying."

"What kind of tests?"

She took a large gulp of beer. "I don't have a metabolism like you think of it. My heart doesn't beat the way yours does. One specialist said I wasn't technically alive." She took another gulp.

"But I've heard you breathing," he said.

"Just habit," she said. "I don't think I actually inhale any air, or if I do, it isn't absorbed."

"Then how can you talk, how can you move?"

He waved his hands at her then let them drop to the tabletop.

"I don't know," she said. "All I know is that I can stay at this level as long as I have the charm and eat at regular intervals."

"But you've spent the weekend at my place," he said.

"I brought shakes with me. Remember the thermos? I told you it was a protein shake. Well, it is. Sort of."

Queasiness rose up from Mitch's stomach. He tasted bile at the back of his throat. He grabbed the beer bottle in front of him and took a large swallow. The cool, familiar taste slid down his esophagus and soothed his stomach. His thudding heart slowed a little but he still felt it banging against the inside of his chest. He'd held this woman, lay with her, made love to her and all the while she was a zombie. Dizziness made him close his eyes. He took a deep breath and waited for it to pass. When he opened his eyes, she sat watching him, biting her lower lips. Tears shimmered in her eyes.

A zombie.

Sharon.

Sharon was a zombie.

That's why she's always cold, he thought. That was why she had that earthy smell. Why a gorgeous girl like her didn't have men swarming all over her, somehow they knew, they sensed it. What was wrong with him that he didn't?

"I think I'd better go." He got fast from the table. The chair tipped behind him then rocked back onto its legs. It scraped the floor as he pushed away from it. His feet skidded on the tile, stumbled and righted themselves as he headed for the door.

Sharon hurried after him. She caught up in the front hall. Her hand reached for his arm but she stopped just as inch before she touched him.

"Mitch, I..."

"I'm... I'll..." He yanked the door open and ran out. The last he saw of her was her hand coming up to her face before she closed the door.

All the way home his thoughts whirled in his head. How could he not have known? How could he have gotten involved with her? How could any of this be real? Was it some kind of sick joke, a way for her to get rid of him without saying it? But she hadn't wanted to tell him. He'd forced her. And as much as he tried to tell himself it was ground beef in the fridge, it wasn't.

It was brains.

He knew it.

He barely slept that night. The sheets still had her scent on them, reminding him of the way her cool arms wrapped around him and pulled him against her cold body. The memory of her sighs drove him out of the bed and into the living room. He huddled on the couch, flipping through late night television. How many times had she curled up next to him here as well? Damn, she was every-where in his apartment. He couldn't escape her.

And he couldn't deny that he missed her.

He grumbled his way through work all the next week, avoiding Brian, avoiding everyone. Lunches he sat in his cubicle and worked. Several times he stayed late into the evening, not wanting to face his empty apartment, face the memories of Sharon that floated into his mind whenever he stopped to let himself think.

Late Friday afternoon, Mr. Granger knocked

on the edge of his cubicle door. "Mitch, can I see you in my office?"

"Uh, sure sir."

Mitch followed the shorter man into his office and waited while Granger shut the door. He skirted around Mitch and settled into his black leather chair behind his desk. He folded his thick fingers on the burgundy desk blotter and leaned forward.

"Have a seat, Mitch."

Mitch sat in one of the metal framed chairs. The back was so hard and upright it was impossible to be comfortable. Just one of Granger's little intimidation tactics. He got the leather chair. The peons got the uncomfortable chairs from hell.

"You've been pulling some long hours this week, Mitch. Not socializing much with the other workers. It's been noticed."

"Well, sir..."

"I'm glad to see that kind of work ethic," Granger went on. "There's too much dallying going on in this department. Your example is appreciated."

"Thanks," Mitch said.

"You keep this up and there could be a promotion in it. At the end of the month is the annual management boat cruise. I want you to be there. Bring someone." Granger pushed a white envelope across the blotter.

"Right sir." Mitch picked up the envelope.

"Now back to work." Granger nodded at him and turned away.

Dismissed, Mitch thought.

He carried the envelope back to his desk before opening it. Two tickets to the management boat cruise, including free dinner and drinks. It was exactly the sort of thing he'd wanted to take Sharon to. Before.

"Hey, I hear you got the big invite." Brian's voice sounded from the entrance to Mitch's cubicle. Mitch spun in his chair. Brian waved a white envelope at him.

"Me too! I can't wait to tell Melissa. She'll probably want to buy a new dress. Any excuse, you know." He chuckled. "And I'll finally get the chance to meet Sharon."

"I don't know about that."

"What do you mean?" Brian moved into the cubicle. His voice dropped. "You and Sharon okay?"

"No. I.... no."

"What happened?"

"I..." Mitch shook his head. He couldn't say it.

"She cheat or something?"

"No."

"You cheat?"

"No!" Mitch twisted away in his chair, facing his computer. "I don't want to talk about it."

"It helps to talk about it," Brian said. "Or drink about it. We could go drink about it."

"Go away, Brian."

"Geez, you're in bad shape. You weren't this bad after Gloria. Come on, let's get out of here and you can cry in your beer."

Mitch felt his friend's hand on his shoulder and it scalded him. He pushed the hand away.

"Go away!"

"Mitch, man, don't be like that..."

"She's a zombie." Mitch managed to keep his voice down although his heart started pounding.

"Hey, you catch me before my vat of coffee in the mornings, I'm a zombie too," Brian said.

"No, she's a real zombie. Cold, smells like earth and has calf brains in her fridge. She's a zombie!"

Brian frowned. "Look. You don't want to talk

about it. Fine. Sit in your cubicle and fume if you want but don't give me some bullshit story."

Brian stormed out. Mitch let him go. Just another way this week was his worst one ever.

He stayed in the office until he could barely focus on the computer screen. Numbers swarm and blurred before his eyes. A headache pounded at his temples and laced across the top of his skull to settle right behind his shoulder blades. He rolled his shoulders, listening to the tendons crack. Sharon always knew exactly where to massage. He could almost feel her cool hands rubbing his shoulders.

The memory jolted him back to his desk. Zombie. She was a zombie. A brain-eating zombie with cold flesh.

Yet he couldn't get her out of his mind and even with the whole zombie thing he still...

Missed her.

Home. Time to head home. Have a beer, watch some TV and get some sleep. After a week of hardly sleeping, he felt like he could sleep the weekend away.

That was one way to deal with it.

He headed for home. Outside the streets glistened with a late evening rain shower. The scent of damp earth reached him as he passed the small parkette at the end of his block. Just a few storefronts away stood his favourite coffee shop. The one he'd met Sharon in. As he passed by, he glanced in and saw the same waitress bending down to take an order from a young man and woman. She had long dark hair that curled over her shoulders.

Like Sharon's. Just like Sharon's.

He walked away. And kept walking.

His brown slip-on shoes moved along. They held his gaze as they carried him along, over the wet sidewalk and cracked pavement. The sidewalk turned to asphalt as he crossed streets. Distantly he noticed that it had started raining again. He felt it beat down on his head, dampen his shoulders and strike his forehead. He kept his gaze on his feet, watching them stomp through new puddles. Over time, he felt a squishiness in his shoes. They had leaked. His socks felt soaked. Water dripped from his hair down his neck. He shivered at the cold touch of it down his spine.

Still his feet kept moving even as the sounds of cars and people faded, becoming intermittent.

Around him, the night deepened and still he walked, staring at his feet, refusing to look up, refusing to see anything. His mind stayed pleasantly blank as he watched his shoes moving forward and back, forward and back. Hours passed or was it days? Maybe weeks and months. He couldn't tell and didn't care. As long as he could keep walking and not thinking.

Finally his shoes stopped of their own accord. He became aware of how his feet ached. His leg muscles clenched and cramped. He almost heard his neck creak as he lifted his head. Rain dripped in his eyes. Thunder rumbled in the distance. A few moments later, lightning lit up the neighbourhood and he saw a row of townhouses in front of him. Red brick, small black awnings over the doors. He stood in front of the end one.

He suddenly realized where his feet had brought him.

Home.

Even as he realized it, his body moved again, carrying him up the three steps to her door. His finger reached for the doorbell before he could stop it. He heard the tinkling chime, muffled through the door. Then nothing.

He didn't even know what time it was. Did zombies really need to sleep?

A few minutes passed before he heard shuffling steps behind the door. A latch pulled back and the door opened. Hallway light spilled out making him blink in the sudden brightness. She was a dark form in front of the light then details of her body coalesced. A blue silk dressing gown held together with one pale white hand, her other hand held the door open. Her thick dark hair tumbled in mess curls over her shoulders. Her dark eyes widened.

"Mitch?"

Her voice purred into his ear. He breathed in her musky, earthy smell.

Her zombie smell.

"I'm sorry," he said.

She opened her cold arms and embraced him.

Later in bed, he studied the small charm she

wore around her neck. Even holding it up to the bedside lamp, he couldn't make out the markings on the medallion.

"What does it mean?" he said.

"I'm not sure," she said. "It's something about stasis. I think it keeps me like this." She splayed her arms, indicating her body.

"Did he tell you what would happen if you didn't wear it?"

"Deterioration," she said. "I would get worse."

"Then we'll have to make sure you always wear it."

Her smile quivered on her lips. "I'm not sure why you're back, Mitch."

"I didn't think I would be," he said. "But I love you, Sharon. Zombie and all."

Tears filled her eyes. Before they spilled onto her cheeks, he put his arms around her and felt her cool body press against him.

She did feel like home.

Sure enough when she learned of the management boat cruise, Sharon insisted on buying a new dress for the occasion. He waited in the living room, checking the time every few minutes. Even on a Saturday traffic could be bad and he didn't want to miss the boarding.

"Sharon, hurry. We have to be there by seven," he called up the stairs.

"I'll be right down." Her voice drifted to him. "Just another minute."

He pulled out the envelope and checked the time again. Final boarding at seven fifteen. Brian and Melissa would be there as well. Mitch had finally had to go to Brian with a story about stress, a fight with Sharon, anything he could think of to explain what he'd said. After a couple of coffee breaks and an evening at a bar, Brian had thawed. But tonight would be the first time all of them would be out together. Just another thing that made Mitch's stomach churn. He doubted he'd be able to eat anything tonight.

A footfall on the stairs caught his attention. He turned toward the door. Sharon appeared. A shimmering dress of dark purple draped over her body, emphasizing the swell of her breasts and hips. Delicate short sleeves exposed the pale skin of her collar bone and shoulders. Her dark hair was swept up off her neck into a soft updo. Stray curls hung beside her face and on her neck.

Mitch felt a pressure in his chest and realized he'd forgotten to breathe.

"Is this all right?" she said.

"You're gorgeous," he said.

She smiled. "For a zombie."

He shrugged. "Well, there's always that."

She swatted at him with her purse, brushing it across his arm. He grabbed her hand and pulled her closer.

"Don't mess my makeup," she said. "I thought you were in a rush."

"Spoil my fun," he said.

They made it to the boat before seven. As they locked the car and Mitch took Sharon's arm, he heard a voice call his name.

"Mitch!"

He glanced over to see Brian waving. He stood next to a tall, slim blond woman wearing a white dress. Her blue eyes looked even brighter in her tanned skin. He became aware of exactly how pale Sharon was in the middle of summer. Even a computer hermit like himself managed to get some sun.

Stop it, he thought. No one is paying any attention to that. He forced a smile to his lips as they reached Brian and Melissa.

"I've been looking forward to meeting you," Brian said as he shook Sharon's hand.

"Mitch has told me all about you," she said. "I hope I measure up for his friends."

Brian laughed. "Mitch should measure up for you!"

The easy laughter eased the tightness in Mitch's stomach. Chatting, they all wandered up the gangplank and headed for the bar.

"It's an open bar, ladies," Brian said. "I suggest we get smashed at company expense and let them drive us home." He pulled out taxi chits and wagged them.

"How'd you score those?" Mitch said.

"Snuck them off Kathy's desk when she wasn't looking."

"Brian has slippery fingers," Melissa said with a wink.

They laughed as Brian tucked the taxi chits

into his jacket breast pocket. He patted them and turned to the bartender.

"A round of drinks, my good man and keep them coming!"

The ten year old scotch burned and warmed Mitch's throat as it went down. Sharon's smile warmed him even farther and released the last tension from his body. It was going to be a good night. He rested his hand on her waist and kissed her cheek.

They managed two rounds of drinks before the cruise started. The buffet was spread out on the lower deck. Sharon nibbled on raw shrimp while moving food around her plate. Mitch balanced a beer and his plate before finding a spot at a nearby table to set his drink down. As he ate, he noticed Brian watching Sharon. Brian raised an eyebrow at Mitch.

Dammit, Mitch thought. He never should have said anything.

"Hey Brian, did you finish with the Decumsey file yet?"

Brian choked on a mouthful of beer and started coughing. Melissa slapped him on the back a few times before he was able to breath again.

"Oh man, don't remind me," Brian said. "That job is hellish. We're supposed to be having fun here."

"Right," Mitch said. "Let's get another round."

"Amen!" Brian swallowed his last gulp of beer and raised his empty glass for more.

That was close, Mitch thought as the bartender collected their empty glasses and set down four more, two beers for the men and white wine for the ladies. Brian collected his glass and presented Melissa with her wine.

"A toast," Brian called out. They all raised their glasses.

"To a fantastic night with friends."

"Here here," Mitch said. He raised his beer to his lips.

"Even the zombie ones." Brian's voice was pitched low, under the swell of music starting to filter in from the dance floor. Brian winked as he took a sip of his drink.

Mitch glanced over at Sharon and found her dark eyes staring at him as she raised the wine glass to her lips. She didn't drink any.

Oh shit, he thought.

"I'm going to check out the upper deck," Sharon said. "Mitch, why don't you come along."

She set her plate of food down. If possible, he thought her pale fingers were even paler clenched around her wine glass.

"Sure," he said. "Let's check out the upper deck."

"That sounds romantic," Melissa said.

Please don't follow, Mitch thought.

"Let's finish dinner first, babe," Brian said.

Thank god, Mitch thought. He could always rely on Brian's stomach to take precedence.

Mitch followed Sharon out of the buffet room and up the narrow stairs to the upper deck. Even with the music filtering up, it was quiet here with the gentle lapping of water against the sides of the boat. While they'd been inside eating, the sun had gone down. Light from the city glowed in the night sky but above it he could see the blackness of space and a few bright points of stars. Definitely romantic, but romance seemed the last thing on Sharon's mind from the grim look on her face as she turned to him.

"You told him," she said. She gripped the wine glass with both hands.

"It was right after I found out," he said. "I didn't know what to think or what to do. Brian's my friend. I confided in him."

"Confided," she said. "My secret, my life. You didn't have the right to spread it around."

"I didn't spread. I just told one person."

"Right, and he's keeping it quiet, obviously!"

"Look, he didn't believe me. He thought it was a joke or something so he's just making fun."

"Making fun of me." Her hands trembled. Wine sloshed over the sides of the glass, spilling onto her hands. "And who knows who else he's said it to."

"I'll talk to him," Mitch said.

"A lot of good that will do." She lifted the glass to drain it.

"Sharon." He reached for her arm. She pulled away before he grabbed her. The glass tipped and the remaining wine splashed down the front of her dress.

"No!" she said.

He yanked out some napkins from his pocket and tried to dab at her dress. She backed away from him as his hand brushed the fabric. The napkin caught on her necklace.

"Wait," he said.

"Leave me alone!"

She jerked away. The napkin tugged, tore but held as she moved. The necklace snapped sending his hand flying back. He heard a tinkle as the necklace dropped to the floor.

"Sharon!"

She rushed away from him. The flowing dark purple fabric melded with the darkening night as she turned the corner at the far end of the deck and disappeared.

Dammit, their first fight. He clenched the napkin and banged his fist against his leg. He should go after her, he knew he should but he didn't know what to say. He shouldn't have said anything to Brian but he'd been so shocked, so confused. It was all before he realized that he didn't care, he'd just wanted her in his life.

He had to make it up to her.

But first he should find her necklace.

He didn't even remember what she'd worn. He hadn't really noticed. A slim silver chain. Barely visible against her pale skin. Now against the darkness of the deck he couldn't see it either.

He dropped to his knees, feeling around with his hands. All he felt was the wood of the deck, bits of peeling paint along the edges, some sliver nipped at his fingers. Nothing silver.

Maybe he should just buy her a new chain and medallion.

Not a medallion.

A charm.

His stomach clenched.

The first scream drowned out the electronic dance music.

He ran. His hand grabbed the railing. He almost fell down the stairs in his rush. His feet slipped and slid as he hurried. As he rounded the landing, a woman came running up, screaming. Her shriek pierced his ear drums like an icicle. She shoved her way past him, losing a high heeled shoe that tumbled down the stairs in front of him. He followed the shoe down.

Mayhem ruled the buffet room. The buffet table had been overturned. Trays of food splattered on the floor, mixing potatoes and spare ribs, salad and fruit salad. Shattered plates decorated the rug like confetti. People huddled against the walls, mouths open, screaming. They shoved and pushed toward the doors. In the centre of the room, Sharon bent over a large man, one of the vice presidents, Mitch thought. Her head yanked up and he saw she was chewing on his cheek. Blood dripped from her chin as she chewed open mouthed. All intelligence was gone from her dark eyes.

He had to get her out of here, Mitch thought, but without the charm would she even know him?

He had to try.

Before he could move, two other men rushed forward grabbing Sharon by the arms. She released the vice president who slid to the floor. He landed face down in a tray of mashed potatoes. His blood pooled inside it like red gravy.

Sharon's hands grasped as if she didn't yet realize she wasn't holding onto the vice president anymore. She swallowed and her mouth opened and closed. Looking for another bite, Mitch thought. Without one forthcoming, a moan issued from deep in her chest. She seemed to realize her arms were being held. The moan became a bellow of rage.

Sharon twisted hard, lifting her arms. The men held on as they moved like rag dolls. She brought her right arm close to her mouth, her teeth snapping. The man shouted and let go. He fell back, landing on his butt, hands sinking into a mound of caesar salad.

In a flash, Sharon leapt on the second man. He screamed as her teeth sank into his shoulder. She chewed her way up to his neck. Blood sprayed as she hit an artery.

Screams filled the room, drowning out the sound of her chewing and the man's pleas for help. People stampeded for the doors. They shoved Mitch back until he hit the wall. Bodies pushed past him. He tried to wade through them, aiming for Sharon, but he kept getting pushed back. Across the room, he spotted Brian and Melissa huddling against the bar, clutching each other.

Mitch edged along the wall, bumping against a table. He yanked the table cloth and folded it several times into one thick, long piece. As the crowd thinned, he stepped forward to where Sharon had cracked open the man's skull and was preparing to feed on his brains.

"Sharon," he said.

Somewhere in the depths of her zombie brain she must have recognized her own name or maybe even his voice. He liked to think it was his voice she recognized. She lifted her head.

He swung the table cloth over her head and face. The thickest part landed in her mouth. She instinctively closed her mouth, chewing at the fabric. He tied it around her head, covering her eyes so she was blinded.

"Brian, help me get her out of here," Mitch said.

Brian shook his head, clutching Melissa.

"Brian, help me! I can't manage her on my own. No telling what will happen if she gets free!"

Finally Brian moved forward to take Sharon's other arm. Unable to see, she seemed more manageable and Mitch was able to lead her up the stairs. On the deck, he pulled her toward the back of the boat. He remembered seeing life rafts there with rope. Maybe if he got her out of here, back to her home where she had brains in the fridge, he might be able to subdue her until he could find another charm.

They manuevered her to the back of the boat. In the darkness, Mitch could make out the rough shape of a dingy. At least he thought that's what it was. He found some rope and started looping it around Sharon's arms, tying them down.

"She's a... she's a zombie." Brian's voice shook.

"Yeah," Mitch said. "Help me get her into the raft."

"Mitch, she's a zombie!"

"Brian, I know but she's a tame one, or was with her charm. I get her another one and she'll be tame again."

"She ate people! She ate them!" Brian's voice squeaked in hysteria.

"Shut up!" Mitch said. "Help me or so help me I'll feed you to her!"

They got her into the raft and Brian helped him lower it into the water.

"Leave her, Mitch, you've got to leave her," Brian said.

Mitch swallowed and shook his head. "I can't."

"For god's sake why not?"

"I love her, Brian. I love her."

Mitch turned away from his friend, climbed over the railing and jumped into the water.

The sun beat down on his head as he stepped out of the refrigerated truck. Mitch checked his watch as he walked around the back toward the gas pump. As usual, his hand automatically tugged on the locked door, making sure it was secure. The lock held. He paused to listen and thought he might have heard a thump from inside but maybe not. He'd just fed her an hour ago and Sharon was always sluggish for a few hours after a good feed.

He nodded at the attendant who ambled out to greet him.

"Hot day," he said.

"Yes it is," Mitch said. "Fill it up please."

The attendant stuck the nozzle into the gas tank as Mitch walked to the front of the truck. He pulled a piece of paper from his pocket and checked it.

"Is it far to the Bayroy township from here?"

"Just down the road about three miles," said the attendant. "Turn left and go another five. You should reach it before night fall."

Mitch nodded. "Great, thanks. Do you know

if they have a garage there? Some place I can plug in my truck? I need to keep it cool."

The attendant shrugged. "You might be able to use power from the motel. Most of these big trucks can last a night on battery power."

"I need to be sure," Mitch said. "My cargo has to stay cold."

The nozzle clicked off and Mitch settled up with the attendant. As he climbed back into the truck, he gave the man a wave and drove off. The engine rumbled and he headed down the road, counting off three miles before turning. From behind him in the back, he heard a thump and a soft moan.

"It's okay, Sharon," he called. "I'm heading to Bayroy now. We'll be there soon. We'll find him, darling. This time for sure and we'll get you a new charm. Everything will be all right. You'll see."

She moaned again and he heard her scratching at the door, the way she always did whenever she heard his voice. He imagined she recognized him and felt comforted.

"It's all right," he said. "Everything will be all right. I'll take care of you, Sharon. I love you."

He turned left and listened to her moan behind him. He wasn't sure but he thought he could almost make out words in her moans.

He thought she said 'I love you too.'

Or maybe it was 'I'm hungry.'

He could never be quite sure.

He twisted around to check the padlock on the door one last time. Locked.

Good. He turned back to face the front. He loved her but he had to be safe.

Just in case.

IN DWARF LAND & CANNIBAL COUNTRY

Three miles out from Dwarf Land and Cannibal Country, Momma's horse stumbled and almost threw a shoe on the cracked asphalt of I57. Trotting up ahead on her own pony, Cora didn't realize it until she heard Seth call out, "Momma!"

She reined her pony in and turned around. Momma lay on the ground. Her horse wandered a few paces away. Seth sat on his own pony, clutching the reins to his chest, his eyes open so wide they took up almost half his face.

Cora clicked her heels into her pony's side and set him trotting back to Momma. As she drew close, Momma sat up, running one hand across her forehead. In the early morning light, Cora saw the scraps on her elbows and one gash on her right leg. Momma stood up, placing her hands on her back to brace herself. She stretched, arching her back.

"You okay, Momma?" Cora said.

"I'm fine, Corabelle," Momma said. "I should have checked old Sidney's shoes before we left the inn, that's all."

Cora glanced around at the empty highway, spotting the rotting hunks of distant cars ahead of them. Just off to the right a ramp curved off to an abandoned gas station. The creaking of the hanging metal sign swaying reached her in the early morning quiet. As she listened, Cora realized she hadn't heard any birds for a while now. Didn't they usually sing in the mornings? She turned back to Momma.

Momma limped as she headed back toward Sidney. She reached for the reins.

"Momma," Cora said. "I don't hear no birds."

Momma missed the reins. She looked back at Cora, her wide eyes reminding Cora of Seth's at that moment.

"What…?"

A howl broke the morning calm. Sidney the horse whinnied in fear, shying away from Momma. A second howl joined the first. This time, the horse reared up, front legs thrashing out in panic. Momma jumped back as the horse landed and galloped away. Cora's pony shook his head. She felt him tremble beneath her and she did what Poppa had always taught her, stay in control and have a firm hand. Horses needed firmness to guide them. She tightened her grip on the reins, letting her pony know she was still boss. But across the way, she could see Seth struggling.

"Momma!" she said.

Momma grabbed the axe from behind Cora's seat and slapped the pony on the rump. The pony jumped and trotted forward, heading for Seth.

"Get out of here," Momma yelled. "Take Seth and go!"

"But Momma, the cannibals!"

"GO!"

She hefted the axe in both hands. Cora saw the metal head glint in the sunlight. From around the ruined gas station, several figures appeared, shambling, stumbling, staggering forward. They wore rags and torn clothes over emaciated, decaying bodies. They moaned and howled as they caught sight of the three people and increased their pace.

"Go, Cora, now!"

As Cora's pony passed Seth, Cora grabbed the left rein out of Seth's fumbling hands.

"Hang on," she said to her brother. The boy nodded, digging his hands into the pony's mane.

Making sure he was secure, Cora took one last look over her shoulder at Momma. She stood in the middle of the road, all five foot three inches of her. Dark brown hair, escaped from the turban wound around her head and tumbled down her back. Her callused hands clenched the axe, ready to swing. Heavy denim pants stuffed in the scuffed leather boots on her feet. The blue shirt now tore and dirty from the fall. Cora imprinted every one of these details into her mind.

The shambling cannibals howled and snarled as they moved toward her. Cora tightened her grip on the reins until the leather dug into her hands. Even from this distance, she could smell the sour, rotting stench on the breeze. How could Momma stand it so close? Why didn't she run?

"Momma!" Seth cried.

Cora jumped in her saddle. Her heart hammered in her chest.

"Cora, go!"

Biting her lip, Cora turned away from Momma, dug her heels into her pony's side and raced away. Seth's pony followed behind. Over the sound of the pony's stomping hooves, she heard the shrieking of the hordes as they descended on Momma.

"I told your Momma she shoulda taken the road past Hemsford," the old man said as he stirred the pot of stew. "157 goes too close to Dwarf Land and Cannibal Country."

"Hush Raymond," the old woman scolded. "Don't be nattering at these children." She passed a rough hand over Cora's head and then over Seth's.

"You'll be fine staying with us for a few days," she said.

"Only a few," the old man said. "We can't be taking you for longer. We don't have the resources for ya." To his credit, he frowned at this pronouncement. At least if he was booting them out, he felt bad about it, Cora thought.

"That's all right," Cora said "I only need one night."

Seth turned to look at her. A lock of dark brown hair fell over his forehead, looking so much like Momma's hair it made Cora's chest hurt. She brushed it off her brother's head and he didn't push her hand away. His lips tightened into a thin line.

They ate huddled in the main room of the old couple's cottage before the old man led them back to the barn. Again he apologized only in his mind as he showed them where to lay their blankets in the empty stall next to their ponies. Cora almost heard him recall his own son as he took a final glance at Seth before leaving them in the barn.

As he closed the door, Seth sat up on his blanket.

"What did you mean you need only one night?"

Cora sighed. "You aren't coming with me, Seth."

"Who says? She's my Momma too."

"Seth…"

"You try and leave me behind, I'll just follow you. You know I can do it, Core."

Now she thinned her lips at him. She did know he could do it, the same way she knew Momma was still alive, deep inside Dwarf Land and Cannibal Country. She felt the spark of Momma inside, pulling at her like a magnet. She hadn't realized that Seth could feel it that way too.

"I'm psycho just like you," Seth said.

Cora shook her head. "It's not psycho, it's psychic, you idiot."

He dismissed her with a wave of his hand. "Yeah, I'll still follow."

Little runt would follow her and then were would she be? Trying to find Momma and having to worry about him following behind her. Might as well bring him along although Momma would be angry. But Momma would be angry anyway. Momma wanted them to keep going and find Poppa down in the island country. But she couldn't leave Momma, Cora just couldn't do it.

"You do what I tell you. Everything I tell you," she said. "Or I leave you for the cannibals and they'll make you their own."

All bravado dropped from his ten year old body. "You won't let them make me one, will you, Cora? Please say you won't!"

Tears shimmered in his eyes, reminding her he was still just a boy. An annoying, stupid, idiot, dolt of a brother but still a boy. Cora put an arm around him, pulling him to her side.

"I won't let them make you," she said. "I promise. Besides, you'd make a better dwarf anyway, short as you are."

He pushed her arm away, but a half smile played across his face. "You're mean, Cora-bora."

"Get some sleep, Seth-beth. We got some riding to do tomorrow."

"Don't call me that."

"Don't you call me that."

"I said it first."

"Oh shut up," she said.

In the morning she tried once more to get him to stay behind but he wouldn't. They argued in silence all through the breakfast the old woman made them of runny porridge and hunks of hard, dark brown bread. It wasn't until the woman waved the pitcher of water in front of Cora's face that she realized the woman was talking to her. She shifted her attention from her brother.

"Are you all right, child?" the woman said. "You were just staring at the wall."

"I'm fine, ma'm, thank you," Cora said. She couldn't explain without causing more questions and more problems. People didn't understand and these days what they didn't understand, they decided to kill first and figure out later, that's what Poppa always said. Don't say anything about the spark, don't say anything about the seeing, don't say anything about nothing. Even Seth, in all his stupid brother ways, knew better than to say anything.

After breakfast, Cora sent Seth to pack up their blankets and she helped the old woman carry the dishes out to the barrel behind the house.

"Just put them down here, child," the old woman said. Cora set them on the wood bench. As she stepped away, the woman handed her a large bundle.

"Take this, you'll need both hands," the woman said.

Cora put out her arms to catch the bundle. The weight of it made her take a step back.

"Don't tell him," the woman said, nodding her head at the direction of the barn where the old man had gone.

"I won't," Cora said.

The old woman smiled but sadness seeped all around her, muddying up her glow as Cora thought of it.

"You sure you want to go out there, child?"

"Yes, ma'm. Thank you. I can't repay you."

"Don't you worry about that." The old woman's rough hand patted Cora's cheek. "You be careful."

"Yes, ma'm."

Cora hurried away, clutching the bundle to her chest. She knew from the woman's thoughts it was stuffed with food; breads, cheeses, dried meat and vegetables. Enough food for her and Seth to last for weeks if Cora was smart about it. And she was smart about it. Poppa had always shown her what to do.

Seth met her by the barn and helped her stuff the provisions into the saddle packs on each of the ponies. It almost made up for losing all the supplies from Sidney's run but it didn't come close to making up for Momma. They'd have to take care of that themselves.

They scrambled onto their ponies and set off back down the road. Clouds hid the sun, plunging the morning into a dull grey that pounded at Cora's temples. She noticed Seth felt it too; he hunched over the back of his pony, wincing at every bump. By mid morning they reached the road to Hemsford and the turn off toward 157. Cora stopped her pony and waited for Seth to reach her.

"Are we going back there?" he said. She could hear the fear creep into his voice even as he held himself steady. Trying hard to be brave for Momma.

"I thought we go 'round," she said. "Come in cross country. They won't be expecting that."

Seth nodded. "Okay."

Heading off the road took them deeper into the country. At first everything looked the same to Cora; the trees, the bushes, various animals that fled from their path – all normal. But as she angled them toward the north, getting closer to Dwarf Land and Cannibal Country, she started to notice small differences. At first the trees seemed to shrink, trunks bending over like old, arthritic men, branches reaching for the ground instead of up into the sky. The leaves looked tinged with a sickly yellow around the edges. The roots bulged from the ground as if the trees were trying to pull up from the ground to run away.

Then she noticed the bushes that looked sunken into the ground, as if some giant had walked across the land, crushing them. Again the same sickly yellow tinged all the leaves. Thin, spindly branches curled along the ground, quivering in the breeze like beckoning fingers.

Soon even the trees and stunted bushes began to diminish in number. Cora noticed fewer and fewer animals crossing their path. The ones she did see looked strange and sickly. One strange long bodied creature that could have been an otter if not for the quivering spines on its back, limped across the ground, turning to hiss at them when Seth's pony got too close. The pony shied away. Even Seth hunched his shoulders as he clutched the reins to his chest. Cora rode up, waving a stick to shoo the thing away. It limped away, legs smacking the ground as it hurried along.

"What was that?" Seth said.

"I don't know," Cora said. "You don't touch nothing here. It's all sick, like Momma said."

The mention of Momma made Seth thin his lips. He turned his head away but not fast enough for her to miss the shimmer of tears in his eyes. She was sorry to upset him but couldn't let him forget why they were here. They had to get Momma.

Cora still felt the spark in her mind, glowing deep inside Dwarf Land and Cannibal Country. As she swayed to the rhythm of her pony's walk, she could almost feel the sparkle grow into an image: Momma stooped in a cage, stunted men around her, poking, prying, and demanding. But Momma couldn't help them. All around the hordes of emaciated, decaying figures shambled in mindless circles, waiting for someone to command them.

Cora shuddered, pulling her attention away from the vision. She noticed Seth up ahead, paused on the top of a small rise. He waved at her. Cora kicked her heels into her pony and they trotted up fast.

"Cora, is it cannibals?" Seth whispered as if the group of stumbling figures in the valley below could hear him. Maybe they could, she thought. No one knew the abilities of these shambling, emaciated creatures that howled and kept coming no matter what weapon you used on them. The only thing that stopped them was burning them into ash or chopping them into pieces. Like Momma with the axe. Cora blinked fast to rid herself of her own tears.

She peered where Seth pointed, down in the valley. Several figures stumbled along, heading in a generally east direction. As they watched, one fell over. The others ignored it and continued on. The fallen one struggled to stand, but one of the legs snapped and it couldn't rise without falling. As the others moved away, the one on the ground began to drag itself along, leaving half a damaged and bloody leg behind.

Seth stuffed his fist into his mouth. Cora heard small whimpering noises come from his throat. She felt her own stomach twist in repulsion. She didn't want to travel down into that valley but it was the quickest way. Would they pass that bloody stump? Would the stump thrash out at them? It couldn't possibly, but those things couldn't possibly be alive after being dead, and if that could happen then maybe anything could happen, like an attacking stump.

"Let's rest a moment," she said to Seth. He nodded, turning away from the valley. She led him to a stunted tree where she tied up both ponies so they wouldn't wander away. After making sure the animals were properly watered and fed, she and Seth sat down on the ground to munch on some of the old woman's hard, brown bread stuffed with rice and vegetables. Cora sipped water from the canteen and handed it to Seth. He took a gulp and then a bite of food. With each chew, his countenance brightened. He smiled at her, his mouth full of food. He opened it wide to show her and moaned.

She yanked the canteen from his hand. "Stop being silly," she said even as she smiled. He stuck his tongue out at her, still with flecks of rice clinging to it.

"You keep that up and I'll pull it out."

He yelped and jumped up, dashing around the tree. He hovered out of sight, peering around the spindly trunk then ducking back when she looked. Cora turned her head away, pretending to ignore him. She sipped more water and finished her small meal. She'd let him play for another few minutes before they started again. A boy should be allowed to jump and run, even in this place.

The ponies whinnied and pawed at the ground. They yanked on their reins. Cora stood up, brushing dirt from her pants.

"Settle down, you," she said.

Something moaned in response.

She spun around as an emaciated figure lunged at her. She managed a scream as it grabbed her arm. Cora tried to jerk away but the boney fingers clutching her forearm tightened and held fast. The stench of its rotting flesh rolled over her, making her gag. It opened its mouth, thin lips pulling away from jagged broken teeth. The tongue lolled out, swollen and black, the skin cracked and oozing. The head bent over her arm, ready to chomp down.

"Noooo!" Seth charged from behind the tree. He swung something that caught the cannibal creature on the side of the head. The ponies' feed bag, Cora realized. The creature let go as it stumbled back from the impact. The ponies whinnied in fear, yanking on their reins.

Burned into ash or cut into pieces, Cora remembered the ways to get rid of the cannibal men. But Momma had taken the axe and all the matches were in the pack on the back of her pony, behind the figure in front of her. She had to get past him.

Seth backed away, clutching the bag in front of him. Cora angled the opposite way, hoping to get around the cannibal man to the ponies. With two of them, the cannibal man swayed back and forth, hissing at each of them in turn, unable to decide which to attack. As Cora moved closer to the ponies from the left, the creature lunged at her again. She jumped back as Seth ran to the ponies.

"Matches," she yelled to him. The cannibal man turned and noticed Seth fumbling with one of the saddle bags. He roared in anger and shambled forward, fingers like claws reaching for Seth.

The boy shrieked and darted away. The ponies stomped and whinnied in fear. White forth whipped from their mouths as they tried to chew through their bits to get away. The creature sniffed and howled. Its hands grabbed the haunch of Seth's pony, nails digging into the flesh. The pony screamed.

"Baybeau!" Seth said.

The cannibal man bit down on the pony. Blood spurted. The pony bucked, shrieking in panic. The reins still held, tying it to the tree. Cora's pony screamed in response, stomping his hooves and shaking his head.

Cora froze. What could she do? She couldn't reach the matches and she didn't have an axe. The creature chewed and chomped on the pony. The pony struggled to get away, but its back legs collapsed. Seth huddled a ways away, clutching the feedback to his chest. He wept as he watched the cannibal man killing his pony.

Cora's heart pounded. Her shoulders hunched with fear and shame. How could this happen? She was the oldest, she was responsible. She was supposed to know what to do and she did, but she couldn't do anything. She'd never felt so helpless, not even when the cannibals surrounded Momma.

The pony fell on its side. The cannibal man ripped a chunk of flesh from the animal's flank. Seth cried out and buried his face in his hands.

Cora had to do something.

Her hands tightened into fists at her sides. Heat swept over her body, starting from her head and swooping down to her toes. Her heart thundered in her ears. The hazy black glow around the cannibal man coalesced in her mind. Flashes of red lightning stormed through it. She felt herself reaching for that red lightning and squishing it with her hands. As she pressed, the lightning flashed up her arms, aiming for her head. She opened her mouth and gobbled it up before it reached her brain. The glow around the cannibal man dimmed. The flashes lessened. After a few moments, they sputtered to a stop.

A gurgling howl reached her ears. Cora's eyes refocused. The cannibal man jerked away from the pony and fell to the ground. His body spasmed, limbs flapping, before the body stopped. The head lolled to the side. His mouth hung open, hunks of flesh clung to his broken teeth. Blood smeared his cheeks and chin. The eyes were wide open and staring.

The pony still struggled on the ground, whinnying in pain and fear. The gash on its back flank bled and festered.

Cora hurried to the pony, leaving a wide path around the cannibal man but he didn't move. She murmured soothing words to the animal, her hands caressing its neck and head. After a few minutes, the pony settled down, snorting, the legs no longer pawing at the earth. Cora still felt it trembling beneath her hands. The gash on its rump oozed. Watching it she knew she couldn't leave the animal to suffer.

"Seth," she said in the same tone as she spoke to the pony. "I need your help."

Her brother looked up, hiccupping. He crushed the feedbag in his arms and rocked back and forth.

"Please Seth."

He sniffled, wiped his arm across his nose, smearing snot across his shirt. He climbed to his feet and scurried over.

"I need you to pet the pony for me. Keep him calm," Cora said.

The animal's eye rolled around to look at Seth as he squatted beside it. He reached out trembling hands to touch the animal's neck. Cora stood up.

"Where you going?" Seth's voice rose high in panic.

"I'm staying right here. I just need to get something. Keep petting him."

Cora moved away, careful to stay in Seth's line of sight. Like the pony, the whites of the boy's eyes shone out at her, conveying his barely suppressed panic. She passed her own pony and stroked its neck, soothing it. It pawed at the ground and snorted as if it understood what she had in mind.

On the other side of the stunted tree, she found a large rock. Hefting it out of the ground took her three tries before she managed to get her arms around it and braced herself. The weight of it almost overbalanced her. She stumbled back a few steps before she could move forward. Seth watched her in silence. His hands still stroked the pony's neck. He probably didn't even realize he was doing it, she thought.

"That's good, Seth," she said and she reached him. "Now turn away."

"What are you gonna do?" His voice still squeaked high, making him sound like a boy half his age.

"I have to take care of the pony, Seth. He's been bit. You know he'll get sick and we can't let him, can we?"

Tears shimmered in the boy's eyes. He shook his head and swallowed.

"Turn away now," Cora said.

"I wanna say goodbye."

"Okay," she said. "Be fast about it."

The boy bent over the pony's head. He planted a kiss on the pony's cheek. "Bye bye, Baybeau. You're a good horse."

The pony snorted. Seth backed away but he stayed facing the pony.

"Seth, turn away," Cora said.

The boy didn't respond. He stared at the pony.

"Seth, do what I said."

Finally, he turned his back. Cora hefted the rock as high as she could then slammed it down on the pony's head. The pony shuddered once, legs flopping, then lay still.

She gathered what she could from its saddle bags and stuffed them into her pony's bags then untied her pony. She led it around to Seth.

"Let's go," she said. "You get on and I'll walk."

The boy climbed onto the pony's back. Cora wrapped the reins around her hand and led him deeper into Dwarf Land and Cannibal Country.

With only one pony, their progress was greatly reduced. With a full sized horse they could have both rode at the same time, but the pony was too small to carry the two of them so always one of them had to walk. From the haunted look on her brother's face, Cora decided to let him ride for the rest of the day. He'd been so proud when Poppa gave him Baybeau. He'd taken the best care of that pony.

As the sun started to go down, Cora knew they'd have to find some place to hide for the night. Around them, the flat of the land stretched out. Stunted vegetation and trees was all she could see. Off to the west, the land angled up into sloping hills that led to the mountains but here in the valley, everything lay flat and squished, as if the gods had stomped everything down. A reckoning, Poppa called it.

Shadows stretched dark, spindly fingers across the hard ground. The bushes darkened to pools of blackness. The trees looked more and more like bent, withered men. Things scurried across their path, just out of sight, seeming to get closer as the darkness encroached. Seth sat hunched on the pony, staring at the ground. He hadn't looked up or spoken in hours. Cora bit her lip. Coming after Momma had seemed vital before but as night fell, fear crept across Cora's skin, making her shiver. She'd already lost Seth's pony and a good chunk of their supplies that she couldn't stuff into her pony's saddle bags. Now she couldn't even find a decent place to set up camp for the night. Poppa had always talked about outcroppings and overhangs, even clumps of trees for protection. But in this stunted, barren land even the trees seemed to shun each other, never growing closer than twenty feet together.

A few more steps and Cora pulled the pony up to a stop by one stunted tree and a cluster of small rocks. At least she could use the rocks to create a circle around a fire and tie the pony to the tree. Her feet throbbed when she stopped walking. They were here for good. She couldn't bear to take another step.

Seth slid off the pony and stood off to one side as Cora gave the animal water and food. Listening to the pony munch on his feed, Cora glanced over at her brother. She didn't like how he just stood there.

"Seth, can you set those rocks in a circle for a fire?" she said.

The boy didn't move. His eyes had a far away look in them. Cora took a breath and opened her mind to him, looking at the glow around him. It was subdued, dull and fractured, not at all its normal blossoming orange. Momma would know how to light up his glow. But Momma wasn't here. Cora had never done anything to a glow herself, except for the cannibal man and crushing the red lightning inside it. She didn't want to think too much about that. Her own ability frightened her more than the darkness. She'd never thought she could do such a thing. It was even more than Momma did.

She couldn't do anything for her brother's glow, was too nervous to try. She'd have to reach him another way.

"Come on, Seth, please? I need your help."

He still didn't respond. His body seemed hunched and stunted like the trees. Was he really becoming a dwarf like she'd teased? No, that wasn't possible. But in the deepening shadows, maybe such a taunt held more power than she imagined. Maybe she would lose him to the stunted, mangled dwarves.

"Seth!"

Still nothing. Tears stung her eyes as she turned and hobbled over to the rocks. They slipped down her cheeks as she set the rocks in a circle and gathers twigs and brush into a pile and lit them with her matches. A thin stream of smoke trickled out as the twigs caught fire. She added more until actual flames began to lick at them. When the fire was good and started, she fetched Seth and led him over to it. Pushing on his shoulders forced him to sit down. Now he stared into the orange light. Even as it reflected and played off his face reminding her of his glow, he still appeared lifeless and lost.

Cora busied herself getting food together, heating some stew from the old woman and handing Seth a cup when it was finished. He sat with it in his lap, staring at the fire. Cora forced herself to eat. Part of her wanted to yell at him, shake him awake. Why did he get to hide like this? Sure he was just a kid but she was only four years older. Why did she always have to be the strong one? She always had to look out for him and it wasn't fair.

The stew tasted like ash in her mouth. She swallowed and felt the lump slide down her throat. The sip of water from the canteen tasted metallic and didn't help much. Seth still hadn't eaten a bite. Cora wanted to slap it out of his hands, slap his face until he cried or screamed or something. She bit her lip hard to stop the impulse. She had to be strong. Poppa had always told her how strong she was, named after coral, one of the strongest things in the sea.

Be strong while I'm gone, Corabelle, he'd said.

She took the cup and spoon from Seth's hands and spooned some into his mouth.

"Eat some, Seth," she said. "It's good."

For a moment, she didn't think he'd respond but then he began to chew. After a moment, he swallowed. She spooned another mouthful into his mouth.

"Eat more," she said.

He chewed again and she continued to feed him. When he dribbled a bit, she wiped it off his chin. He took a few more bites then stopped opening his mouth. She tapped the spoon to his lips but he wouldn't open.

"Come on, Seth, finish."

Nothing. What more could she do? She didn't want to waste the food. She took a bite, chewing slowly. Another idea formed in her mind.

"Hey Seth, what do you think of this?"

She saw his gaze flick toward her. She opened her mouth wide, showing him the chewed food. He blinked. For a moment, the ghost of a smile flittered across his face.

"You can't do that," she said.

His lips quivered, flattened and then relaxed. She held up the spoon to his mouth. After a moment he opened up and she slipped the food inside. He chewed, his eyes fixed on the flames in front of him. Then his gaze slid back to her. He opened his mouth and stuck out his tongue.

Cora laughed. The ends of Seth's lips curled upward. She spooned more food for him. After a few times, he took it from her and finished up himself. As he licked the spoon, she ruffled his hair and kissed his cheek. He squirmed away.

Just like Seth.

She set out blankets for them and tucked Seth in. He fell asleep before she sat up again. Lying on his side, his hands curled into loose fists, his dark hair falling over his forehead, he reminded her of the baby he'd been so long ago. She brushed sand from the blanket and kissed his forehead.

"Sleep well, Seth," she said as quiet as she could.

Then she sat up, back to the tree and facing the fire to see if anything evil came out of the darkness.

Something nudged her shoulder. Cora blinked. Fuzzy shadows blurred in her vision. Her muscles felt stiff and lethargic.

"Seth, what…?"

Her vision cleared. Light from torches danced around her. She spotted hulking, hunkering figures standing in a rough circle around her. At her side, stood a squat, misshapen man, his overlarge head tilted precariously on narrow shoulders. His thin arms, one shorter than the other, ended in large hands. He held a gun in one of them and he used it to poke her shoulder again.

"Awake now, deary?" he said in a deeper, gruffer voice than she expected.

Fear made her muscles clench tighter. One of the dwarf men! She'd heard the dwarves commanded the cannibal men but she'd never really believed it until now and seeing the emaciated, swaying figures holding torches around her. She stared back at the dwarf and swallowed.

"This ain't no camp ground for you," the dwarf said. "What are you doing here?"

"Lost," was the only thing Cora could manage.

The dwarf frowned. The flickering light deepened the lines of his face, giving him gargoyle features.

"I don't think that's true," he said. "You're

an awful deep way into our territory to be lost. Maybe I should ask the boy?"

He turned to his left. Cora followed his gesture. Seth stood between two emaciated figures, each holding one of Seth's arms. The boy shook, barely standing on his feet. Cora saw the wet spot on his pants.

"Let him go!" she said.

"You tell me the truth first, deary," the dwarf said. "What are you doing in my land?"

Cora's hands gripped her knees until the knuckles turned white. She felt the pinch of her fingers on her skin. The pain helped focus her, brought her anger boiling to the surface and washed out the fear.

"You don't have to scare him," she said. "He's just a little boy."

The dwarf laughed. His head fell back and for a moment, Cora thought it would roll off his neck and onto the ground. Then it came forward again. The dwarf wiped at his eyes.

"You're feisty, deary, I'll give you that." He nodded. "I like it. Don't see many feisty ones here." He took a step back and waved a hand. Two rotting cannibal men stepped toward her, hands reaching. Cora tried to scramble to her feet but her stiff muscles refused to work fast. By the time she got to her knees, the cannibal men were on her, thin fingers wrapping around her arms and dragging her to her feet.

"If you ain't going to answer my questions here, maybe you'll answer them at home," the dwarf said. "Let's go."

He turned away and began a limping, hopping walk. The cannibal men shambled after him, dragging her and Seth along. Cora turned her head to see Seth but in the darkness, she only caught glimpses around the hunching figures.

"Seth," she said. "It'll be all right."

Her brother didn't reply and she wondered who she was trying to reassure, him or herself?

If felt like they walked for hours through the darkness. Could the little dwarf man walk that far? At one point, she caught a glimpse of some animal ahead, a pony or a small horse. He was probably riding that, leaving her and Seth to be dragged along with the cannibal men.

As they stumbled up a steep rise, Cora noticed a lightening of the sky. Was it already sunrise?

The air still felt too cold for dawn. As they cleared the top, she saw distant lights. A town lit up in the darkness. Her shoulders hunched. The skin along her back tightened. Those lights weren't fire but something strange and ancient, from the before time, before Dwarf Land and Cannibal Country. Evil omens, her Poppa would say. No one survived seeing those lights.

The cannibal men dragged her forward. She had to move her feet or let them be scraped along the ground. With every step, her heart pounded faster. Her body trembled but the cannibal men tightened their grip, bony fingers digging into her biceps. She had to breathe through her mouth to avoid the worst of their stench. As they got closer to the city, the group drew closer together. The smell of rotting flesh and decomposing clothes hung heavy in the air. She heard Seth coughing behind her, off her right shoulder. She tried to twist to see him but the cannibal men jerked her back to face forward.

"It's okay, Seth," she called out.

Her brother didn't respond but she heard the dwarf laugh. She felt blood flush her cheeks in anger. She narrowed her eyes, focusing ahead. In the darkness, she saw the shimmer of a silvery blue glow. Dark slashes of purple raced through it as the dwarf chuckled. That was his glow, she thought. She'd remember that.

They soon reached the outskirts of the town. Cracked asphalt roads led them past crumbling ruined buildings. Some of them Cora recognized as houses, short single buildings that tilted to one side or sagged on their foundations. Other buildings she never seen the likes of before, tall structures that stretched into the sky, disappearing into darkness. Dark windows faced out like blind eyes but she could feel the energy of all the lost, dead people within, vibrating and churning. Her skin crawled. Her muscles jumped under her skin as if they wanted to leap away without her. The cannibal men tightened their grip and dragged her forward.

The road opened up to an open air square of concrete. At the far end a large rectangular, shallow trough sat with several beams arching over top. Cora couldn't understand what those arches were for, some kind of covering, like a tent? But why over a trough, if that shallow box was a trough? Did they have that many horses in Dwarf Land and Cannibal Country? She couldn't see how. Horses were expensive, even their ponies cost a lot and proved Poppa's wealth since he could supply both his children with ponies. If the dwarf men had that many horses, surely they wouldn't be so shunned.

But she didn't see any horses, just more cannibal men shambling around. Several dwarves shepherded groups of the emaciated figures across the open square. The dwarves shouted and smacked the figures with long sticks that sparked as they struck the grey, mottled skin. Whiffs of burning flesh tickled her nostrils but the cannibal men seemed impervious to it. They moaned and continued moving in ragged, faltering lines.

A yell halted the cannibal men dragging her. As they stopped, Cora tried to pull away but they gripped her hard. She twisted around, trying to catch a glimpse of Seth. She spotted the top of his head behind her to the right, obscured by several other cannibal men.

A thud in front of her drew Cora's attention. The dwarf stood beside his small horse, brushing off the front of his pants. He motioned at another dwarf who ran off into the darkness. Voices and sounds of a scuffle followed.

At the edges of light, several cannibal men appeared, dragging a figure toward them. Cora thought it was another cannibal man from the torn clothes and ragged hair hanging across the face. Then the head moved, exposing a slice of cheek and nose. Cora felt her mouth drop open in shock.

"Momma!" Cora lunged forward, dragging the cannibal men with her for several steps. They howled, pulling at her, almost in separate directions. She felt the sockets of her arms stretch and cried out at the pain.

"Stop that!" The dwarf man snapped one of the silver sticks at the cannibal men. They stopped yanking at her and just held on. Cora sagged between them. Tears of pain streaked her cheeks. She blinked, trying to clear her blurry vision and see Momma. Momma's head lolled. Her bare feet dragged behind her as the cannibal men brought her forward. When they let go, Momma crumpled to the ground.

"Let her go!" Cora said.

The dwarf man laughed. "You're quite the feisty one, aren't you? Maybe she'll pay attention to you." He stepped away from Cora and headed for Momma. His hand aimed the silver stick and he prodded Momma with it. Cora winced, but there wasn't any telltale spark. He'd turned it off.

A groan sounded and Momma rolled onto her back. One hand brushed her hair from her face in short, jerking movements. Cora saw blood on her mouth. One eye was swollen shut. Even her glow, normally a vivid, rich blue, was streaked with sickly orange and yellow.

"Wake up," the dwarf said. "Look what I found wandering in our lands."

Momma's one open eye focused on the dwarf and then shifted past him to rest on Cora. Cora bit her lip. Momma had told her to take Seth and get them away. She'd failed at her task.

A tear slipped down Momma's cheek, streaking the dirt.

"I thought they might be someone you recognized," the dwarf said. "Feel a little more cooperative now?"

Momma's lips thinned as she pressed them together. How many times had Cora seen Seth copy that same look? She knew what it meant, same as it always meant when Seth did it. Seth had learned his stubbornness from a master.

The slight shake of her head made the dwarf scowl. He shook the stick at the cannibal men. They shambled forward, reaching for Momma. Even in her weakened condition, Momma struggled. Her leg kicked out, hitting one of the cannibal men in the knee. His leg snapped. With a groan, he fell forward. His face hit the ground. Thin fingers scrambled at the dirt. But already another rotting figure took his place, reaching for Momma. There were too many to fight. Multiple hands clutched at Momma and lifted her up off the ground.

"You saw this coming," the dwarf said. "You and those other seers. What happens next? How can we get out of this mess?" He waved the stick and this time it crackled in the air. "Talk!"

"Can't." Momma's voice croaked out the word. Saliva dribbled down her chin.

"What do you mean 'can't'?" The dwarf man slammed the stick at the ground. It sparkled and hissed. The cannibal men holding Cora moaned at the sound.

"Can't talk, won't talk? What do you mean?" the dwarf said. "You see who I have here? You want me to use this on her?"

He pointed the stick at Cora. She stared at the end of it, glowing a faint red like a hunk of burning coal. Cora shivered, her body pulling away from it but she could barely manage an inch. The cannibal men held her fast.

"No," Momma moaned. "Can't see. Can't see anything no more." She gasped at the effort of her speech. Her head hung forward, her hair falling to cover her face.

The dwarf grabbed Momma's hair and yanked her head up. "You're lying. You saw this coming. I want to know what happens next. You're going to tell me."

Even in his gruff anger, Cora heard the fear in his voice. The dwarf man was afraid, afraid of what might happen next, afraid of Momma because she used to be able to see. What he didn't know was that Momma has lost that ability years ago. It faded away, Momma had called it, and said it was a relief. She hadn't liked seeing what she saw: the plagues sweeping across the lands, the cannibal men rising from the numerous dead, the horrific radiation that turned normal men into stunted, twisted creatures like this dwarf man. All of it faded from her Vision and she'd been glad of it. A lightness had come over her, bringing smiles and laughter, driving away the thinned lips, hunched shoulders and weeping in the night when Momma thought no one heard her. But Cora heard it. Cora had seen the shift in her glow from the beautiful blue to a darkness almost black. But when the Vision faded from her, Momma was set free.

Until now.

A sob shook Momma's body. Cora watched streaks of black crack through the blue of Momma's glow, like reverse lightning. Momma was trying to see, trying to resurrect that lost ability. Cora struggled against the hands grasping her but couldn't break their grip. No Momma, don't do it, Cora thought. The effort would only hurt her.

Momma's eyes rolled up until all Cora could see were the whites. Her body shook from effort.

Red froth dribbled from the corners of her mouth and down her chin.

"Momma, no!"

Momma didn't hear her. She shook so hard the cannibal men lost their grip and she fell to the ground, limbs jerking and flailing. As Cora watched, the black lightning streaking across the blue of Momma's glow expanded, gobbling up the blue into emptiness and nothingness. Cora knew if it covered all of the blue glow Momma would die.

Tears blurred Cora's vision although not her ability to see the glow. The one thing she wished would blur and it never would. She was starting to understand what this was, this ability to see glows and what she'd done to that cannibal man. She remembered focusing on the flashes, pulling them in and gobbling them up. She'd done it because she'd wanted it. She'd made it happen.

The tears shimmered and blurred everything in her eyes, making the lights shift and dance. Her heart pounded in her chest, sending blood roaring through her veins and in her ears, like the thunder howls of the cannibal men as they shrieked in unison, rising up against the dwarf men. Mighty stomps shook the earth as the cannibal men stomped and bashed down the dwarf men and broke through the boundaries of Dwarf Land and Cannibal Country to sweep across the earth, howling their rage to the sky. A hand pointed and the cannibal men moved; it pointed elsewhere and the cannibal men spread that way, following the hand that pointed, the mind that directed. The one that saw.

A boy's cry cut through Cora's vision. She blinked, coming back to the world.

"Momma momma momma..." Seth's voice babbled over and over.

In front of her, Momma lay still on the ground. She'd stopped convulsing, Cora saw. Relief flooded her. Maybe now Momma would be okay. Except Momma didn't move. Nothing, not even a rise and fall of her chest for breathing. The dwarf man crossed his arms over his narrow chest, walked up to Momma and kicked her head. Her head lolled over. Blank eyes stared up toward the dark sky, at nothing. Cora's stomach clenched as she allowed herself to look for Momma's glow.

Blankness.

"No!" She screamed.

"Oh shut up," the dwarf man said. "Useless child. I knew we should have drugged her deeper. She did this on purpose."

The dwarf man's nattering rambled in her ears, devolving into noise. Behind her, she heard Seth weeping. In front of her, a steady drip of blood fell from Momma's lips, staining the ground beneath her. Cora stared at the growing puddle, saw it expanding to cover the square, the city, all of Dwarf Land and Cannibal Country before extending to the world. With every drip, the vision became clearer to her, with every drip the coal of anger smoldering inside her burned brighter.

"They rise up," she said.

The dwarf man nattering stopped. "What?"

"They rise up. The cannibal zombie men rise up. They listen and rise up."

A smile twisted the lips on the dwarf man, one side rising higher than the other, looking lopsided on his face. "Looks like I pushed the wrong seer," he said. "Keep going, girl. I want to know what else you see."

"They rise against the stunted masters, rise and spread across the land like that." Cora nodded at the blood pooling beneath Momma's face.

"How?" the dwarf man said. "How do they do this?"

Cora shook her head. She wouldn't tell him. He didn't deserve to know.

The dwarf man scowled at her. "Tell me," he said. "Tell me or I'll take it out on the boy."

"No," Cora said.

The dwarf man snarled. Before Cora could say another word, he skittered forward and lashed out with the stick. It struck Seth across the face. He shrieked. The stench of cooking flesh filled Cora's nostrils. She screamed. Seth sagged between the cannibal men holding him. She couldn't tell if he was dead or unconscious.

"Stop!" Cora said.

The dwarf man paused, holding the stick high in the air. "Are you going to talk?"

She nodded.

He lowered the stick. "Good. Then tell me. How do they rise up?"

"They listen," Cora said.

"Who do they listen to?" said the dwarf man.

Cora let the slow smile spread across her face. Around her, she saw the glows of all the cannibal men. She sent her thought out among them, felt the lightning grow and grow in her mind as she pushed it outward, felt the cannibal men turn toward her...

"They listen to me," she said.

Hands fell away from her arms and shoulders. Surprise widened the dwarf man's eyes. His mouth opened in an O. He stumbled back several steps as the cannibal men who had been holding Cora moved forward. A shuffling noise from behind him made the dwarf man turn. He lifted his stick.

"Stay back!"

He waved it, hitting grey, peeling flesh that hissed and bubbled and stank of burning where the stick struck but still the cannibal men shambled forward. Cora saw the lightning energy flow over them. She lifted her hand and pointed...

...at the dwarf man.

The cannibal men fell on him. He screamed, arms flailing, the stick sparking before it was struck from his hand. It skidded away in the dirt. The screams grew louder, echoed across the city as Cora pointed and pointed, sending lightning colors over the cannibal men, sending them to do her bidding.

Soon the screams turned to gurgles as the cannibal men overwhelmed their masters and began to feed.

As the cannibal men shambled around her, Cora bent over Seth. Her fingers touched his face and neck, searching for the throb of his heart beat beneath his skin. Cool, it felt so cool to her finger tips. A blanket, she needed a blanket to keep him warm. Then he would be all right. Everything would be all right. She lifted him into her arms and cradled him. She knew she had to protect him from the lightning all around. The glows burned fierce with raging lightning. It spread through the cannibal men like wildfire, igniting them in a frantic fever.

Cora bent her head over her still brother and waited for the storm to rise and sweep across the remains of Dwarf Land and Cannibal Country before spilling over to engulf the world.

About the Author

Based in Toronto, Canada, Rebecca M. Senese writes horror, science fiction and mystery/crime, often all at once in the same story. Garnering an Honorable Mention in "The Year's Best Science Fiction" and nominated for numerous Aurora Awards, her work has appeared in *Tesseracts 16: Parnassus Unbound, Imaginarium 2012, Tesseracts 15: A Case of Quite Curious Tales, Ride the Moon, TransVersions, Deadbolt Magazine, On Spec, The Vampire's Crypt, Storyteller, Reflection's Edge, Future Syndicate* and *Into the Darkness,* amongst others.

When not serving up tales of the macabre, mysterious or wondrous, she volunteers as a zombie or vampire at haunted attractions in October to stalk and scare all the unsuspecting innocents.

Find Me Online

Website - http://www.RebeccaSenese.com
Twitter - http://twitter.com/RebeccaSenese